THE FALSE CHILD

LM Kaplin

THE FALSE CHILD

LM KAPLIN

Broken Brain Books

Some children belong to the mound

CHAPTER 1

The second hand of the clock ticked like a countdown to freedom, its slow, deliberate movements mocking the students of Room 203. The children were restless. Mrs. Hargrove's voice droned on, reciting another algebra lesson, her enthusiasm waning as much as her audience's. Summer vacation was a mere five minutes away, and although the students were lethargic, the potential energy in the room felt electric, like it could explode at any moment.

Rather than pay attention to their teacher's lecture, most of the students stared out the windows, lost in their daydreams, eager for their imminent release from the brick prison that confined them. There might have been only a few minutes left in the school year, but Mrs. Hargrove continued to ramble about solving for Y in a two-variable equation as if a test was in the class's near future.

The only thing Ethan saw in his immediate future was a horde of zombies. With his brand new copy of

Undead Uprising 4 being delivered that afternoon, he had trouble keeping his mind on anything else. He had waited months for the game's release, which the publisher surely planned to coincide with the start of summer break. After raiding the pantry when he got home, he planned to lock himself in his room for a marathon gaming session. If Ethan had his way, he would spend the entire summer playing video games.

"Pssst," a voice hissed from behind him, breaking his thoughts. "Ethan."

He turned to see one of his classmates motioning toward the door.

"Your sister," the boy whispered.

Ethan looked toward the hallway and saw his older sister, Julie, waving at him like a lunatic. Her lips moved dramatically as she mouthed something he couldn't understand. Her wild hand signals did nothing to clue Ethan in on her message as he shrank lower in his seat out of embarrassment. He glanced up at the clock and saw there were three minutes left before the bell rang. He shrugged his shoulders at her and pointed to an imaginary watch on his wrist, then held up three fingers before breaking eye contact.

Visibly frustrated, Julie's head disappeared from the window.

"Is there something in the hallway more interesting than my lesson?" Mrs. Hargrove asked, interrupting her lecture and glaring directly at Ethan.

"No. Sorry, Mrs. Hargrove," he replied, straightening his posture and attempting to look engaged in the lesson.

A few snickers escaped from the back of the room at the reprimand. Ethan resisted the urge to turn his head and glance at the offenders. He knew the likely culprits without needing to move a muscle. The last thing he cared about was the opinions of Noah Cahill and Connor Stevens. Although they didn't quite rise to the level of class bullies, he would be happy never to see either of them again.

Just as the teacher returned to her lesson, a black blur smashed into the classroom window, causing half the students to jump in their seats as the glass shuddered from the impact. A collective gasp filled the room as a magpie slid down the pane, leaving a faint streak of blood before crumpling into the bushes below.

The entire class was on its feet, craning their heads for a better look.

"Ew!" someone squealed.

"Did you see that?" another said. "It came from the hill!"

"The orphanage," whispered a boy near the back.

The mere mention of the word spread murmurs across the class like wildfire.

"I heard it's haunted."

"My brother said kids went missing there."

"My dad says it's full of rats the size of dogs."

Mrs. Hargrove clapped her hands, her voice louder than usual. "Everyone sit down!" The chatter died as the kids returned to their seats, but the unease lingered. She smoothed out her skirt and forced a smile. "Birds fly into windows all the time. It's nothing to be frightened of."

But Ethan noticed her eyes drift toward the hill, just for a moment. The orphanage waited there, a dark mark in the bright summer sky. He had been warned to stay away from the abandoned building his entire life, as had every other child in Fairfield. They had all heard the stories of missing children and rumors of evil creatures. But the structure sat empty and fenced off their entire lives, leaving most to consider the tales nothing more than a scare tactic by their parents to keep them away from the derelict building.

Ethan had no interest in breaking into some smelly old building, anyway. If he wanted to go exploring, he would fire up his console and play the latest dungeon crawler. Even his parents would agree that playing video games was safer than wandering into an abandoned building that looked like it could collapse at any moment. He would have to remember that one the next time his mom told him to turn his game off and get some fresh air.

Finally, the bell rang, its shrill tone startling the already uneasy class. Chairs scraped against the linoleum as kids jumped from their seats and a stampede of feet fought their way for the door.

"Don't forget your summer packets!" she called after them, her voice lost in the chaos.

Mrs. Hargrove watched as her students shuffled out of the room. They rarely thanked her and never looked back. She knew that was just how kids were, but she couldn't help feeling a sense of attachment to them. She cared for each of them as if they were her own. As she grew older, it seemed she became more attached each year.

Who could blame her for having a little extra empathy for the children of Fairfield? She was in her first year of teaching when the misconduct at the orphanage came to light. Then, with those poor girls going missing so many years later, the town had been through more than its share of heartbreak. But that was a long time ago, and in the end, it brought their tight-knit community even closer together.

Mrs. Hargrove held back a tear as she watched the students file out of the room. None of them knew it, but it was her final year of teaching at Fairfield

Middle School. She decided to hold off announcing her retirement until after the semester let out. The children struggled with their grades enough without one more thing to distract them from their studies.

The classroom emptied quickly, with only a few stragglers left behind, including Ethan, who sat at his desk packing up the last of his things. By the time he stepped into the hallway, Julie stood just outside the door with an impatient look on her face.

"So, are you coming to the game?" she asked. "We should be halfway to the ball field by now."

Ethan groaned. "I already told you no. I've got plans."

"Plans to sit in your room and play video games all day?" she shot back. "You'll have all summer to stay holed up in your cave. One day of socializing isn't going to kill you."

She had a point. It was their first summer not being shipped off to Blue Rill Day Camp, a place they had both come to dread over the years for its early morning start times and jam-packed schedule of crafts and activities. The freedom felt strange, almost too good to be true. With the siblings getting older, they had successfully lobbied their parents for a summer on their own terms as long as they promised to look after each other and stay out of trouble. All it took was a few months of begging, pleading, and being on their best behavior for their parents to agree. At thirteen years old, Ethan considered himself more than capable of looking after his own needs. Some cultures consider thirteen a grown man, after all. While he didn't love the idea of being attached to his sister's hip all summer, it beat the alternative of being dunked underwater in that murky excuse for a lake by the kids at camp.

Julie looked up at her brother, her eyes narrowing. "Come on, it'll be fun. Everyone's going to be there."

"Exactly," Ethan muttered.

Julie stopped in front of him, forcing him to halt. "Maggie's going to be there," she said, a mischievous tone in her voice, as if taunting him.

Ethan froze, his cheeks turning red. "So what?" he mumbled, looking away.

Julie smirked. "Oh, come on. You've been crushing on her since you were in diapers. This is your chance to impress her."

"By what? Striking out?"

Ethan couldn't deny he had a major crush on Maggie. He had since before he could remember. Maggie Evans was his best friend growing up. Living across the street from each other and sharing a bus stop, they had always been a part of each other's lives. The pair had been inseparable throughout elementary school and around the neighborhood. But the past year had been weird for their friendship.

Ethan developed feelings for her, but Maggie made it clear that their friendship would remain exactly that and nothing more. He accepted the fact that he had been relegated to the friend zone and buried his affection, but he couldn't change how he felt. Although he was content just kicking back and killing zombies together like the old days, she seemed less interested in hanging out with him recently.

Instead, she was spending time with Noah and Connor, of all people. Ethan wouldn't have been surprised to learn she was dating one of those idiots. Either way, he didn't know what she saw in them. To him they were just a couple of cookie-cutter jocks with zero personality and even fewer brains.

The last thing Ethan cared about was the baseball game, especially knowing those two would be there. He would rather be home playing *Undead Uprising*. He was about as athletic as a salmon in a three-legged race, but he had to admit it would be nice to see Maggie. Maybe he would have a chance to wiggle his way into her summer plans. Plus, he knew Julie had already made up her mind and wouldn't take no for an answer.

"Well?" she asked.

Ethan hesitated. If he played his cards right going to the game could change the whole trajectory of his summer, but playing baseball—especially with Maggie watching? That was a whole other level of pressure.

As if reading his mind, Julie spoke up. "No one cares if you're good," she said, rolling her eyes. "Just show up. Besides, Noah's pitching. I know you don't want him getting all of Maggie's attention."

Since they had grown apart, Ethan spent less time attempting to impress Maggie, but he hadn't given up on their friendship yet. "Fine," he muttered at last, shoving his hands into his pockets. "But if I strike out, I'm blaming you."

Julie grinned. "Deal."

She knew her brother didn't want to play and that half the reason he agreed was for her benefit. It wasn't fair that her parents placed more limits on her than on Ethan. She was a year older and a million times more mature, but dragging her brother with her was easier than convincing her parents she was old enough to go alone.

The siblings exited the school and made their way toward the back of the building, where the ball field sat sandwiched between the middle and high schools. The shared athletic fields minimized costs for the town and created a central spot for locals to gather and watch the games.

Next to the campus, on a hill overlooking the town, sat the abandoned orphanage. With the orphanage housing many of the town's children, constructing the schools on the empty lot nearby seemed a straightforward decision at the time. The thought was it would make attendance more convenient for the children who lived there. Instead, news of the scandal at the orphanage broke soon after the schools' construction, forcing the facility's closure. Since then, the building loomed over the town as a constant reminder of the misdeeds committed within. Some even said the headmaster's ghost still roamed the halls, begging for forgiveness.

It took years for the town to recover from the scandal, but just as the people had begun to move on, tragedy struck again when a group of local children last seen heading toward the orphanage went missing. The loss still festered in the minds of those old enough to remember, such as Mrs. Hargrove.

Residents advocated for tearing down the building, but just before the bulldozers moved in, the state intervened, preventing the planned demolition. With the officials' hands tied, the town sealed the orphanage and erected an iron fence around the property. The added safety measures and stern warnings from parents across town had kept out prying eyes and curious children, but it didn't stop the rumors and speculation from running wild around town.

Fairfield Gazzette

Early Edition   Fairfield's First Choice for News Since 1926   Vol. 32 No. 10

50¢

June 4, 1975

FAIRFIELD CHILDREN'S HOME OPENS ITS DOORS

With a ribbon-cutting ceremony attended by Mayor Harold Jenkins and Reverend Maurice Cole, the new Fairfield Children's Home officially opened atop the northern hill overlooking town.

"Every child deserves a fair start in life," declared Headmaster Patrick Brennan, whose tireless fundraising and anonymous benefactors made the home possible.

The three-story brick structure will house up to fifty orphans from across the county, providing discipline, moral guidance, and a proper education.

Townsfolk have already dubbed the newly constructed building *Fairfield Manor*, praising its grand windows and commanding view of the valley. The mayor said he expects the orphanage to be a defining landmark for the small town and a hub of activity for decades to come.

CHAPTER 2

As Ethan and Julie turned the corner of the building, they spotted Maggie not far ahead of them, a bat slung over her shoulder. She was chatting and laughing with Connor, while Noah trailed behind them, throwing a ball in the air and then catching it. Just last year it would have been Ethan walking side by side with her. Instead, she was flirting with those dickwads. Ethan felt his blood boil with anger and jealousy at the sight of them together.

Of course the popular kids, who happened to be on every sports team, who could have their pick of any girl in the school, had to take an interest in his best friend. Noah's father was the town sheriff and man-around-town, so everyone was always kissing his ass and offering him favors to win points with his dad. Even the teachers let his assignments slide when any other student would have received a failing grade.

The only time either of them paid Ethan any mind was to laugh at his expense. Needless to say, he avoided them whenever possible, but he knew a confrontation at the field was inevitable. He just hoped they wouldn't embarrass him in front of Maggie. He quickened his pace to get within earshot of the trio to listen in on their conversation.

"I don't think I'll be able to make it. My family is going on vacation to Myrtle Beach that week," said Connor.

"Well, I guess that's your loss," replied Noah. "My parents are going all out for this one. I'm talking a live DJ, a make-your-own ice-cream sundae bar, and a shit ton of fireworks. My dad's friend in the fire department is gonna set it all up, so you can bet it'll be legit. You know my pops. Anyway, it's gonna be a blast!"

"I'll be there for sure," said Maggie. "It sounds fun, and I'll be around all summer."

Suddenly, Connor's beach vacation didn't sound so hot if it meant he would miss the biggest party of the year. "Maybe I could stay with you while my parents are away?" he suggested. "I don't want to be stuck down there with them, anyway. My dad will be playing golf with his buddies all day while my mom gets drunk on cheap wine. It's kind of boring, actually."

"That should be fine, but I'll have to ask my folks," Noah replied.

Maggie noticed Ethan and Julie trailing them and slowed her pace, allowing them to catch up.

"Hey, Ethan, I'm surprised to see you coming this way. Are you gonna play in the big game?"

Ethan glanced at his sister, who returned his look. "Yeah. Well, Julie wanted to play, and we've gotta stick together, so I didn't have much of a choice. But I'm feeling lucky today. I think I might hit a home run," Ethan replied confidently.

Connor and Noah burst out laughing at the remark. They were well aware of Ethan's nonexistent athletic prowess from years of gym class and recess together.

"I'll take my chances with Julie on my team," Noah proclaimed, goading the other boy. "She's more likely to get a hit than you."

Ethan grimaced even though he knew Noah spoke the truth. The other boys continued laughing at Ethan's expense as they picked up their pace and jogged down the hill, away from the group. The kids gathered on the center field had already begun separating into teams.

Maggie looked at Ethan and motioned toward the field. "Let's go. We don't want to miss getting picked for a team."

Ethan knew it might be his only opportunity to talk to Maggie without the other guys overhearing the conversation, and he didn't want to miss his chance to invite her over. "Hey, Mags," he called after her. "Do you want to come to my house and kill some zombies after the game? I got the new *Undead Uprising* waiting at home. It just came out today."

Maggie looked back at him without slowing down. "It'll probably be too late by the time the baseball game is over."

Ethan's heart sank as the words left her lips, and he realized his plan of inviting her over was nothing more than a pipe dream. He suddenly regretted agreeing to play in the game at all.

"But maybe tomorrow?" she added as she ran down the hill, still looking backward at Ethan. "That sounds like fun."

Ethan regained a sliver of confidence, and the hint of a smile spread across his face. Maggie smiled back and turned away, speeding off down the hill. A raincheck was better than nothing. Maybe going to the game wasn't such a waste of time after all.

But just as Ethan's morale had been brought back up, Noah was there to crush it. By the time Ethan and Julie reached the center of the field where everyone was gathered, the teams were already selected. When Noah spotted the siblings joining the group, he made a show of calling for Julie to come to his team and sending Ethan to the other, repeating his lame joke to a larger audience.

Of course Maggie was on the team with Noah, Connor, and Julie, leaving Ethan to fend for himself. Even if they were seriously outmatched, at least he knew a few of the kids on his team. It wasn't like Ethan cared who won, although losing would just be one more thing for those assholes to rub in his face.

Inside the orphanage, a presence stirred. The creature had been waiting for years—watching and listening. They had seen children come and children go, leaving only their footprints and the faintest traces of their scents behind. But as the sounds of the game drifted through the boarded-up windows, they felt a new urgency in their quest. With their numbers dwindling since the orphanage's closure, they knew it was almost time to venture out again in search of fresh vessels in which to take root.

The creature carried themselves silently through the crumbling halls, their form seeming to shift with each step in the darkened room. Their pale features gave off a radiance as they crept, transforming the shadows and illuminating the decayed remnants of rotting furniture and abandoned belongings with a pale-green hue. They stopped by a window and peered out a small opening in between the boards. They observed the group of children playing on the field below, oblivious to Fairfield Manor and the hungry eyes watching them from the shadows, waiting for their chance.

Abandoned and sealed shut since before their birth, the orphanage was an afterthought in the children's minds, blending in with the overgrown brush surrounding it. To the boys and girls of Fairfield, the old building was just another piece of the landscape.

Hidden in the background and forgotten was usually the way the manor's inhabitants preferred it, left alone from outsiders and prying eyes. But it had been many years since they had welcomed guests into their home, and the time to venture out was at hand. Finding new candidates was no easy task, and a calculated risk would be required. Their declining numbers required action, even if that meant inviting humans and the inherent danger they brought with them back to their doorstep. And while they were loath to risk exposing themself by entering the human world, they grew bored inside their prison.

It was almost as if the nice folks of Fairfield tempted them by constructing the school right in the manor's shadow. So they waited, and they watched the children play, knowing that soon the orphanage would open its doors once again and they would welcome new visitors with open arms.

The creature's yellow eyes focused on Ethan and Julie. It sensed their bond, the unspoken connection between siblings. Bonds like theirs were rare and powerful—perfect for what it needed. Soon it would set its plan in motion, and before long, they would return to their realm with a prize for their kin.

The creature feared the idea of venturing into the human world and the prospect of being discovered, but it had returned to the abandoned halls out of desperation, tasked with ensuring the survival of their kind. All they needed was the right moment to step into the children's lives unnoticed.

Their form shifted again, almost taking on the shape of a boy. They studied the kids' faces, mimicking their mannerisms. Soon, they would join the children. Soon, they would be one of them.

Outside, Ethan laughed nervously as he took his turn at bat, his team cheering him on. The creature's lips curled into a faint smile. It wouldn't be long.

As the sun sank lower in the sky, casting the long shadow of the orphanage over the field, the game continued, the children blissfully unaware of the danger lurking just beyond the wrought-iron fence.

CHAPTER 3

Gene Bell picked up the half-empty can of cheap beer sitting on his workbench and pressed it to his lips. The fluorescent lights hanging overhead in his garage reflected off the top of his balding crown as he tipped his neck back, taking a large swig of the lukewarm beverage. Gene released a weary sigh as he placed the can back in its resting spot and looked over the plans for his current project.

Even after procrastinating on the set of chairs he had been building for over a week, he lacked the motivation to finish the job. The customer who commissioned the pieces already called twice, asking when the furniture would be complete. The first time, Gene had given him the runaround, telling the man he had to find the perfect wood for the job. On the second inquiry, Gene told him the chairs were finished and just needed to be stained. The truth was he only had the pieces cut for two of the four chairs, never mind beginning the assembly. The parts lay on a rusted metal shelf next to his workbench, and Gene didn't give one iota. He had half a mind to cancel the order altogether. The only thing stopping him was that he already spent the deposit on some groceries and the case of beer sitting next to his mini-fridge.

The roughly cut pieces were far from his best work. Truth be told, he hadn't built anything worth a damn in the past decade. Long gone were the days of intricately carved cabinets with lattice doors singing of fine craftsmanship. Creating something beautiful with one's own hands required a sense of pride in their work, and any satisfaction Gene got from his pieces had long since evaporated.

His wife leaving was the last nail in his coffin. She was the only thing holding him together after the girls went missing. He didn't blame her for packing up and moving away. The pain of staying in that town, in that empty house, and reliving those awful memories every day was too much for her to bear. She had lasted as long as she could. If Gene was smart, he would have gone with her, but the possibility never even crossed his mind. There was nothing left for him in Fairfield, but he stayed regardless, holding out hope for his daughters' eventual return even though he knew in his heart they never would.

It had been ten years since his wife moved to Arizona, five years after Sarah and Liz's disappearance. They kept in touch at first, but over time, their calls became less and less frequent. She was determined to leave the past behind and move on with her life. If it was only that easy for Gene. He couldn't let go; he didn't want to. Even though he knew his girls were gone, he had to stay. The thought of them returning home to find a strange family living in their house left no other option.

Gene stretched his knees as he stood up from his workbench and looked out the window of his garage, glancing down the road at a group of neighborhood kids playing baseball. He resented their laughter, and he hated himself for it. They weren't to blame for the tragedy that befell his family so many years ago, but seeing everyone else move on with their lives while his daughters were left behind prevented the hole in his heart from healing.

Gene thought to himself that his twin girls should be out there playing in that game, nevermind the fact that fifteen years had passed since their disappearance and they would be much older, probably off starting families of their own. In Gene's mind, Sarah and Liz would remain fourteen forever.

He finished the rest of his beer and grabbed another from the case, tossing the empty on the floor with the rest of the discarded cans. Shuffling his feet, he returned to the window and popped open the beverage.

He used to know all the local kids when his girls were in school, but he could hardly name any of them anymore.

When the girls first went missing, the town rallied around Gene and his wife, dropping off meals, helping around the house, and doing their best to be supportive neighbors. The search parties kept the couple's hopes up at first, but their faith diminished when the long hours of combing the area for days on end produced no results. Eventually, Gene retreated into his shell and just wanted to be left alone. The worst part was the lack of closure. With no bodies or proof of death, they couldn't even hold a proper funeral for the girls, leaving him in a state of constant sorrow and uncertainty. It was enough to break anyone.

Even with no definitive answers, Gene had little doubt about what happened to his daughters. He placed the blame for their disappearance squarely on one boy and, by association, his mother. All their troubles began when the girls started hanging around Billy Wilkins. They had never been interested in boys before that, but Gene knew they were getting older, so he held his tongue when he noticed their new friend hanging around more often. He even refrained from voicing his concerns about their change in behavior whenever they were around the boy. They were both suddenly in love with Billy, when the week before they had barely given him the time of day. If Gene had only trusted his gut and spoken up about the squirrelly glimmer in the boy's eye, maybe he could have stopped the twins from going out that day. Maybe things would have turned out differently. Maybe they would still be there.

When the girls failed to return home for dinner that night, he knew right away something was wrong, but his wife reminded him what it was like at that age and brushed it off as kids losing track of time. By sundown, she had changed her tune and they were both sick with worry. When morning arrived with still no word from the twins, he headed to the sheriff's house at first light.

Driving up to the two-story brick colonial with an immaculately manicured lawn, visitors would have guessed the home belonged to a doctor, lawyer, or even some tech bro who hit it rich and retired to the countryside, not the local small-town sheriff. But it was no secret that Bruce Cahill happily took kickbacks in exchange for a promise of a favor down the road, and everyone wanted a favor from the town sheriff.

When Bruce's wife answered the door, Gene quickly explained the situation, and she fetched her husband.

Together, the men went out in search of the missing girls.

Gene insisted their first stop be Billy Wilkins's house. He knew his girls had been spending most of their time with the boy, but when they arrived to question him, his mother, Eliza, claimed her son had gone missing as well. While the sheriff considered the possibility that the trio ran away together, Gene didn't trust the calm manner in which Eliza spoke of her son's disappearance. He became convinced she was hiding something. Since then, his distrust of the woman grew until it festered into an uncontainable hatred. In his mind, Billy Wilkins killed his daughters, while Eliza helped the boy dispose of the bodies and skip town. Even without any evidence of her involvement, it was the only explanation that made sense to him.

"She knows something," Gene muttered to himself. "She always has."

He drained the rest of his beer and hurled the empty can across the garage. As he reached for another, he caught sight of the double-barrel shotgun mounted above the tool rack. For a long moment, he stared at it, the muscles in his jaw twitching.

Before he realized it, his stool screeched back across the cement floor and he was on his feet, reaching for the gun. The weight felt natural in his hands. The feel of it only increased his body buzz. He opened the barrel, slipped in two shells from the box sitting on the shelf, and snapped it shut with a loud click. It was time to find out what really happened to his daughters.

The crunch of loose gravel outside brought him out of his daydream. Hearing the sound of tires rolling up his driveway, Gene froze, glancing at the shotgun in his hands. When a set of emergency lights came into view, he cursed under his breath.

"Speak of the devil," he muttered.

Gene shoved the gun back onto its hook just as the sheriff's double knock rattled the side door. "Yeah. Come in," he yelled across the garage.

Sheriff Bruce Cahill threw open the door and entered, sporting his customary uniform of a khaki, button-down shirt and matching pants with his signature cream-colored Stratton covering his thinning hair. Bruce's athletic build and commanding posture gave off an intimidating aura. Although the man was only a few years younger than Gene, he could easily pass for half Gene's age. One glance at the two men made it clear who spent their free time at the gym and who stayed home working on their beer belly.

"Hey, buddy," Bruce said, casual as ever. His eyes were drawn to the weapon on the rack before returning to Gene's face. If he noticed the shells gleaming in the chamber, he didn't mention it.

Sheriff Cahill was one of the few residents who hadn't written Gene off as his depression deepened and he morphed from a grieving father into the angry alcoholic he had become. Even though Gene spent more nights than he could remember locked up in the drunk tank down at the station, the sheriff was always nice to him, feeling partially responsible for the unsolved disappearance of Gene's daughters. The fact that Gene's family never received the closure they needed to move on weighed heavily on Bruce. That feeling of culpability was why the sheriff still came by to check on Gene. With such a high-profile case still unsolved after over a decade, it was the least he could do.

Bruce made his way through the cluttered garage, stepping over discarded beer cans and avoiding stacks of assorted wood. "Hope you don't mind my intrusion."

"I don't need you stopping over to babysit me," Gene replied bitterly. "The only reason you still come by is out of pity and obligation."

The sheriff removed his hat and shook his head. "Sorry, pal, but you're way off the mark this time," he replied with a smirk on his face. "I'm not here to be your therapist, but I guess that comes with the territory. I'm here to see my boy, Noah. He's playing in the game down the road. Pitcher. You know how kids are—embarrassed with their parents hanging around and all that. I figured your garage had the best view of the field while staying out of sight. You mind sharing one of those beers with me while we shoot the shit?" he said before surveying the scattered parts on the workbench, "Unless you're busy with something...," he added.

Gene hardly believed the sheriff's reason for stopping over, but he wasn't about to turn away a drinking partner, rare as they were. "Help yourself," he said, motioning toward the case. "But they never made it inside the fridge."

Bruce bent down to retrieve a beer and cracked it open. After an awkward moment, he attempted to fill the silence with the usual small talk. "Did you see the Sox game last night? I can't believe they blew a five-run lead in the 9th. I threw the remote and cracked the TV. You should have heard the shit my wife gave me. It's not like I can't afford another one."

"Nah, I'm not much interested in sports these days," came the reply.

The only sport on Gene's mind recently was a classic game of Russian roulette. The threat of landing himself in eternal damnation was the only thing that prevented him from pulling the trigger. The thought of loading up his shotgun and taking the law into his own hands sounded like a better proposition. It wasn't like he had anything else to lose. If staring down the end of a double-barrel was the only thing that could convince Eliza Wilkins to talk, then so be it.

Gene knew his daughters weren't coming back, and he doubted Billy Wilkins would ever show his face in Fairfield again, but his fury had been building for fifteen years. He was no closer to moving on than he had been on the day of their disappearance. If it was too late to save his girls, he would have to settle for punishing those who wronged them. With the boy long gone, that burden fell to his mother. She would pay for her role in taking his girls away. He vowed that one day the truth would come out. That promise was the only thing that kept him going. But for the moment, he sat back and opened another beer while he waited for a sign.

CHAPTER 4

Even with the children keeping a strict score of the game, Ethan didn't care who won. As long as he didn't make a fool of himself on the field, that was all that mattered. If he struck out against Noah, that would just be one more thing for his classmate to rub in his face. He had plenty of practice ignoring the taunts, but he preferred if Maggie and Julie weren't there to witness the ridicule. Especially Maggie.

Ethan adjusted his stance in the batter's box and squinted his eyes for a better view of the pitcher. He watched the windup as the pitch came in, and he gritted his teeth, gripping the bat tightly. He stepped forward, preparing to swing, but the ball came in high and tight, almost buzzing his chin. Ethan stumbled back, losing his footing as the catcher laughed and threw the ball back to Noah. He had half a mind to throw his bat to the ground and charge the mound, but he knew any display of aggression would only end in his further embarrassment.

Instead, he sniffed his nose and spat on the dirt in front of home plate before preparing for the next pitch.

If somebody asked any of the kids who were there that day what happened next, they would have gotten a variety of answers, ranging from blind luck to divine intervention. Almost none of them thought Ethan, or anyone, could hit the ball that far on their own. One boy even said he saw a bird catch the ball and fly off with it. Regardless of how it happened, the next pitch set off a chain of events that affected everyone on the field that day.

Ethan adjusted his stance, trying to ignore the mounting pressure. Noah wound up for the pitch, his movements exaggerated for show. The pitch was a heater, right down the middle. Noah challenged him with a fastball, confident Ethan's feeble swing couldn't catch up to it. The ball came flying toward Ethan so fast he barely had time to react. He closed his eyes and swung the bat with all ▯his might. A loud crack echoed throughout the field, causing birds to fly from their perches atop nearby trees. Somehow, he hit the ball dead center, sending it barrelling through the air. The ball traveled impossibly far. It went up and over the heads of the outfielders, who turned in comically slow fashion, shielding their eyes from the sun's glare as they followed the ball's path.

For a moment, there was stunned silence. Then someone shouted, "Whoa!"

The hit's long arc stretched high above their heads, and when the ball reached its peak, a sudden gust of wind took it even farther. The ball sailed over the iron fence of the old orphanage, making a perfect entry into an open window on the second floor of the abandoned building.

Forgetting about the unthinkable distance the ball traveled, the chance of it landing inside the open window would have been a million to one. With the children amazed at the spectacular feat, none questioned why a window was open in a building that had been sealed shut their entire lives. They were too amazed at the thundering home run to notice such trivial details. Even Ethan was so taken aback by his performance at the plate he forgot to run the bases.

"Nice going, Danvers," said Noah, taking a menacing stride toward home plate. "I hope you're gonna pay for that ball."

Ethan lowered the bat, his excitement fading. "It was an accident."

"Yeah, well, accidents cost money," Noah snapped, stepping closer. "That ball's gone unless you're dumb enough to go get it."

A few of the kids exchanged nervous glances, their eyes darting between Ethan, Noah, and the orphanage. No one spoke, but the tension was clear.

"Whatever, I'll pay you back for the ball," Ethan offered, hoping to defuse the situation.

Noah shook his head, a cruel grin spreading across his face. "Nah, I changed my mind. You're going in there. You hit it; you go get it."

Julie stepped defiantly in front of Ethan. "Leave him alone. It's just a ball."

"Yeah? That was a league ball, and those aren't cheap," he said. "What's the big deal? You scared of a little old house?"

"We can't go in there," Ethan replied incredulously. "It's gated off."

Noah took another threatening step toward him before Connor intervened in an attempt to calm his friend down. "It's fine. We've got plenty of balls," Connor said in a hushed tone. "That one was nothing special."

Noah glared at his friend for stepping in. Everyone knew his anger didn't come from the lost ball but from the monstrous home run Ethan hit off him. The sheriff's son took another step forward and might have thrown a punch at the batter if Julie hadn't been standing between them. The sight of her with her arms out in a protective stance in front of Ethan caused Noah to stop mid-stride and rethink his actions.

"Whatever," he said. "I'm not going to beat him up over a stupid ball. But he doesn't have to be such a pussy about it and hide behind his sister."

"If it's so easy to get in there, then why don't you go get it yourself?" Julie offered.

Noah balked at the suggestion. "I would, but it's not worth the hassle," he replied nonchalantly.

Maggie watched the interaction, hesitant to pick sides between her friends. But the scuffle had diminished her appetite to finish the game. Relieved that Noah had backed off, she turned to Ethan, who looked embarrassed by the situation. She knew if they stayed the rest of the game would be marred by the interaction.

"You ready to get out of here and go kill those zombies you were talking about?" she asked.

Ethan's eyes lit up at the offer. "You bet," he exclaimed before looking to Julie for approval. He couldn't leave her at the field.

Julie saw the pleading look in her brother's eyes and knew she couldn't let him down. She didn't feel like playing ball anymore, anyway. She ran to the bleachers to grab her backpack. "Let's get out of here."

After collecting their things while ignoring Noah's glares, the trio headed off down the road in the direction of their houses, leaving the game and the argument behind. The laughter and cheers of the other kids resumed but quickly faded into the background as they crossed the grassy expanse, the orphanage looming like a dark cloud overhead. For the first time since he could remember, Ethan watched the orphanage as they made their way down the street. He couldn't keep his eyes off the old building, thinking about the ball he hit.

"Sorry to ruin the game," Ethan said quietly, his shoulders slumped.

Maggie shook her head. "All you did was hit a home run. Noah can be a real jerk sometimes."

"She's right," Julie added. "And you hit that ball farther than anyone. Don't let him ruin that for you."

Ethan managed a small smile, but his gaze lingered on the orphanage. As they walked away, the wind carried the faint sound of old wood creaking in the distance. Ethan shivered, looking away and focusing on the path ahead.

"I wasn't afraid, ya know."

"What?" Maggie asked.

"To go inside the orphanage."

"Oh," she said. "It doesn't matter. There's nothing in there, anyway."

"I just didn't want to go in for that asswipe."

"Yeah, well, Noah takes these games a little too seriously. He thinks everything is a tryout for the major leagues. Sorry about that."

"It's not your fault," Ethan replied. "Although I guess it might be Julie's for making me go to that stupid game in the first place."

"Hey!" Julie exclaimed. "That's not fair. It didn't take much convincing. Plus, you smashed that ball! I mean, you hit it really far. You completely embarrassed Noah.

He won't make the high school team giving up home runs like that to you. No offense." She looked at Ethan to see how he would react to her playful jab.

He ignored the comment. "Yeah, well, that didn't stop him from turning it around and calling me a pussy for not going to get it."

"I didn't see him rushing in to get it, either," Julie replied. "That place is creepy. People say those missing kids are still inside."

"I doubt that," Ethan replied. "The police searched the orphanage, right? If those kids got hurt or lost in there, they would have found something."

"Well, what do you think happened to them, then?"

"I don't know. The boy they hung around with probably killed them."

"So you believe that crazy hermit down the road?"

"Well, considering none of us were even born back then, I really don't know. But it sounds more plausible than anything else I've heard. Ghosts or alien abductions? Give me a break," Ethan said, laughing.

The children continued on their way, laughing as they disappeared down the road, unaware of the presence watching from the hill. If they had, they might have quickened their pace as they walked past the overgrown fence surrounding the orphanage grounds. They might have kept their eyes on the road ahead instead of lingering on the darkened windows of the old building.

But as it were, the seed was planted and the creature's plan was already taking root. Curiosity, once sparked, was difficult to snuff out. The boy would return, the creature was certain.

With a final glance, they slipped back from the window and into the depths of the orphanage. All that remained was to wait, and they had plenty of practice with that.

Fairfield Gazzette

Early Edition   Fairfield's First Choice for News Since 1926   Vol. 32 No. 10

June 18, 1979

50¢

PARENTS DENIED ACCESS TO CHILD AT FAIRFIELD HOME

A Fairfield couple is demanding answers from administrators at the Fairfield Children's Home after being told their daughter was "no longer in residence."

According to Mr. and Mrs. Leonard Price, they placed their eight-year-old daughter, Rachel, at the Home last year while recovering from financial hardship. When they recently returned to reclaim her, Headmaster Patrick Brennan informed them the girl had been legally adopted several months prior.

The Prices insist they never signed consent forms for adoption. "They told us she went to a good family out of state," Mrs. Price said tearfully. "But they won't tell us where or who they are. I just want my daughter back."

When reached for comment, Headmaster Brennan called the situation an unfortunate misunderstanding, stating that proper records exist but cannot be released without approval from county offices.

A spokesperson for the Department of Child Welfare confirmed they are reviewing the documentation.

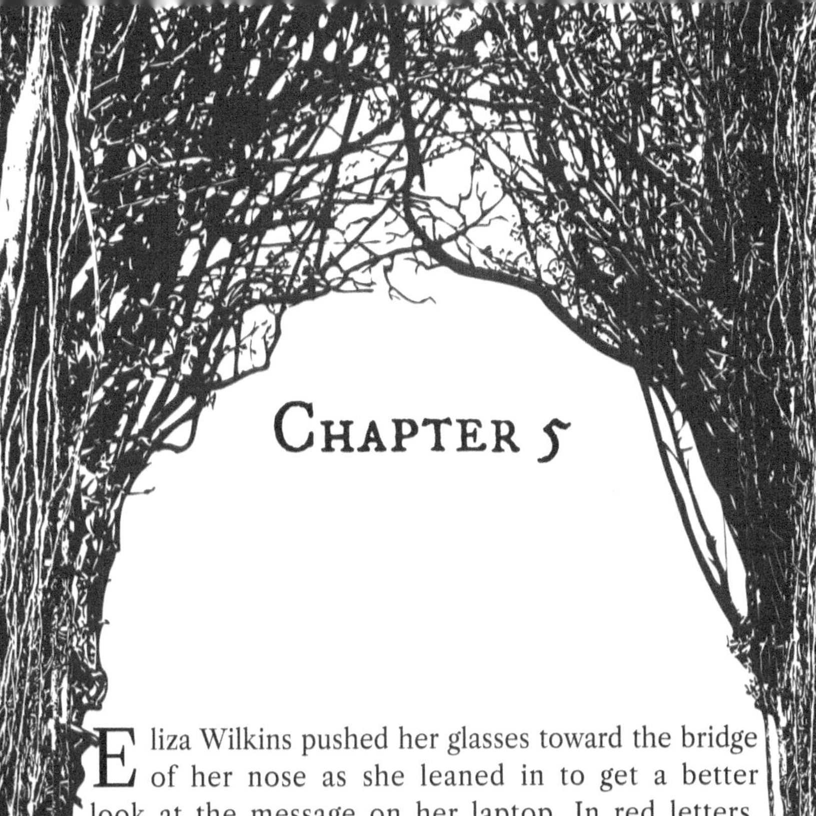

CHAPTER 5

Eliza Wilkins pushed her glasses toward the bridge of her nose as she leaned in to get a better look at the message on her laptop. In red letters, the pop-up box said Please Fix Shipping Profile to Continue. Eliza sighed. Every time she tried to list an item for sale, the screen displayed a new error. She'd about had it with that damn computer. She clicked on the error, and the shipping information window opened. Apparently she missed the section for international orders. She unchecked the box, disabling overseas orders altogether, and clicked Save. The last thing she needed to worry about was a customs officer taking a closer look at her shipments.

Although her packages contained nothing illegal, many of the items would surely raise eyebrows. Her more mundane products, like skin ointments or protection salts, could be explained away, but the totems made from animal bones and the hand-bound spell books would be harder to justify. After her previous interactions with the law, she preferred to avoid giving them any reason to come snooping around in her affairs. They had done enough of that already.

Eliza's Miracle Cures and Ointments had gained quite the following on social media. The limited availability of many of the required ingredients for her tinctures ensured her products sold out almost instantly after listing them. The problem was navigating the website to get them up in the first place. As she struggled to complete the listing, she thought that the creators of the website couldn't have made the form any more complicated if they had tried. Computers were never Eliza's strong suit. She avoided them like the plague for as long as possible, but after rumors about her spread through the town and business in her shop dried up, a friend suggested she open an online store, selling her crafts to a wider audience.

At first she refused. Her reluctance wasn't just about technology; it was about control. In her shop, she could vet her customers, ensuring they weren't getting in over their heads with what they purchased. The anonymity of the internet unnerved her. So she cited the need for personal interaction with her clients, preferring a meaningful connection to her local community. But as time went on, the customers who used to fill her shop looking for anti-aging creams, fertility potions, and her various selection of elixirs disappeared. Gene Bell's false rumors about her and her son drove much of the townsfolk away.

The accusations spread quickly. Whispers of witchcraft circulated through the village, and her once loyal customers stopped coming. Funny how the townsfolk didn't mind her charms when used to their benefit, but one slanderous rumor and she was suddenly grinding up children to use in her potions. An allegation such as that in a small town had an immediate effect on her business, and she soon found herself struggling to get by. Eventually, she gave in to her friend's suggestion and opened the online store. She had little other choice. By a stroke of luck, her store became an immediate success. Although some of her creations could be dangerous in the wrong hands, for the most part she offered concoctions that could be peddled to strangers with little risk.

While the town focused on Gene's loss, they ignored the fact that her son, Billy, had disappeared as well, leaving Eliza to fend for herself to make ends meet. And with Gene's awful lies planted in their heads, there was nothing she could do to change their minds. Because of him, the entire town blamed her poor son for the disappearance of those girls. She saw it in their eyes whenever she crossed their paths. If they only realized that Billy was just as much of a victim as those girls.

She wanted more than anything to clear her son's name, but who would believe he had gone missing days before the Bell twins vanished when he was spotted with them on the day of their disappearance? No, the sheriff would've never accepted her story.

To Gene, her claims of innocence were futile. He had found her son guilty in his mind before she even answered the door that morning. Nothing she said would've changed his verdict. So instead of relaying a truth they wouldn't have believed, she feigned ignorance and sent them on their way with nothing to show for their visit.

Maybe Gene was right. Maybe it was her fault his girls went missing. She knew something was wrong with her son, but what could she have done? She hadn't guessed the truth until it was too late. It took years of obsessive research and chasing down ancient folklore to learn as much as she could about the creatures that lived in the orphanage. She knew the responsibility to prevent further harm, her only recourse, fell to her. So she set her mind to ensuring they remained sealed inside the building's crumbling walls.

Leaving the town had crossed her mind many times, but like Gene, each time, she dismissed it. The orphanage might have taken her only child, but there were others that still needed saving. If not for her, then who else would protect the children of Fairfield? So she stayed in a town that despised her to save the offspring of the people who hated her. With nothing else to live for, she remained determined not to let it happen again.

But time had a way of dulling even the sharpest fears. Nearly fifteen years had passed since the iron fence was built, and with no activity to speak of, she had grown complacent. For years she patrolled the perimeter daily, burning sage and reciting incantations of protection. But her visits became less frequent as the years wore on, and even she began to believe the danger had passed.

While she sat at her dining room table, which hadn't seen a proper dinner in ages, packaging jars of hair regrowth cream and bottles of love potions for her customers, Eliza remained blissfully unaware of the changes unfolding at the orphanage. If she had, she would have certainly dropped what she was doing and scurried over to the property in an attempt to prevent the forces inside from breaking their seal.

Because at that very moment, twisting vines with roots that ran deep underground burrowed their way through the earth with surprising strength, pressing forcefully against the iron fence separating the orphanage from the rest of the world. After years of relentless growth, the creeping plants pulsed with an otherworldly life force, their movements snakelike as they pushed against the man-made barrier. The integrity of the fence gave way, and a bolt fell to the ground. It hit the dirt with a faint thud, joining a small pile of fallen fasteners that had gone unnoticed in the underbrush.

Eliza paused in her work and looked up, a shiver running down her spine. For a brief moment, she felt the air shift, and a sense of worry gnawed at the back of her mind. In her younger days, that would have been enough to send her into action, but she shook it off, blaming her overactive imagination. She returned to her work, but deep down, a small, nagging voice whispered that the fight she thought had ended was about to begin again.

"Dude! Don't go that way. You'll die for sure!" yelled Ethan, his eyes bulging and a look of panic spreading across his face.

Maggie reversed course just in time to save herself from certain death, thankful for her friend's warning.

"This way. Follow me," he said before heading off on the opposite path.

"What's so bad about that direction?" she asked, curious about her friend's dire warning.

Ethan shook his head and laughed. "The moment you step inside the supermarket, the doors close and a million zombies jump out," he said. "It's impossible to make it out alive without some advanced weapons that we haven't unlocked yet. We'd have to reload from the last checkpoint, which would send us pretty far back."

"How do you know all that? Didn't this game just release today?" she asked.

"I already watched DirkPlayz do a full run through on his YouTube channel. The developers sent him an early copy."

"Doesn't that spoil half the fun?" she asked.

"Nah, it's like planning for a dangerous mission," he replied with a grin.

"Well, I hope you don't plan on staying inside playing video games all summer. There's more to life than killing zombies."

"You're starting to sound like my mom. Besides, won't you be off playing baseball with your stupid boyfriend?" he replied sarcastically.

Maggie gave him a playful shove. "He's not my boyfriend. And no, not just playing baseball, silly. There are plenty of things to do around town. We used to love riding our bikes down Main Street, or swimming at the lake, even meeting up at the park to play tag."

"Don't you think we're getting a little old for tag?" he asked.

"You're never too old for tag!" she replied.

"ETHANNNNNN, DINNERRRRR!" The sound of Ethan's mom yelling up the stairs interrupted their conversation.

"Be right down, Mom," he yelled back.

After the pair of zombie hunters reached the next checkpoint, Ethan reluctantly turned off the game, wondering how long it would be before he would get a chance to play with Maggie again.

"I guess I should be going," she said.

"Aren't you gonna stay for dinner?" he asked hopefully.

Maggie considered the offer, knowing her mom was serving leftovers again. "Do you think your folks will mind?"

"Please. My mom will be offended if you don't try her lasagna. I guarantee she's already set a place for you."

"Okay, you talked me into it," she said with a smile.

With the issue settled, they headed downstairs to the dining room and sat at the prepared table.

"Thanks for having me for dinner, Mr. and Mrs. Danvers," Maggie said through a mouthful of food. "The lasagna is delicious."

"Of course. You're welcome over anytime. You know that," Ethan's mom replied.

"So, Maggie, we haven't seen you around much recently," Mr. Danvers said. "What have you been up to?"

"I've just been busy with school and soccer practice, but now that summer break has started, I'm sure you'll be seeing more of me."

Ethan held back his elation at the prospect of spending more time with Maggie over the summer. With the pleasantries out of the way, he waited for a pause in the conversation for the opportunity to change the subject.

"So you know that old orphanage up on the hill?" he asked.

Mrs. Danvers froze, her fork still in her mouth, a look of concern washing over her face at the mention of the abandoned building. She had never seen Ethan show any interest in the property before, which was how she preferred it considering its sordid history.

"Yeah. What about it?" his father replied, curious where his son was going with the question.

"There was a window open on the top floor today," Ethan remarked.

"That's strange. I thought the city boarded it up," his mother replied, looking to her husband.

"They did," said Mr. Danvers. "Are you sure about that?"

"Yes," said Ethan confidently. He wanted to boast of his big hit in the game but knew the idea that he hit the ball that far was preposterous.

As if reading his mind, Julie took the cue and ran with it. "Ethan hit a home run over the fence today," she exclaimed. "The ball landed right inside the window."

"Now I know you're pulling my leg," said her dad. "Even a professional ball player would be hard-pressed to hit the ball that far."

"He did, Mr. Danvers," Maggie cut in. "I don't know how, but he did."

"You should have seen the look on Noah Cahill's face! He was ready to punch Ethan's lights out," added Julie.

Mr. Danvers grimaced at the thought of his son being assaulted by the sheriff's son. "Well, maybe the sun's glare made it seem like he hit the ball that far, but either way, it's strange that the window would be open."

"Well, I hope you kids don't go anywhere near that old building. It could collapse at any moment," Mrs. Danvers told the children, repeating the same warning they had heard their whole lives. She turned to her husband with a concerned look on her face. "Maybe we should have sent them to camp this summer after all. It's not too late to sign them up."

A look of panic came over both Ethan's and Julie's faces at the mention of the C word.

Seeing the fear in their eyes, Mr. Danvers came to their rescue. "Relax, honey. They're fine," he said. "They didn't go near the orphanage, and they know to stay away, right kids?"

"Right, Dad," they said in unison, wearing matching angelic smiles.

"I know this is a big change for both of you," Mr. Danvers continued. "You're not used to having this kind of freedom. But I'm counting on you to watch out for each other this summer. I mean it. If one of you gets in trouble, you can both expect the same punishment."

"Awww, Dad," Julie protested. "That's not fair."

"Life isn't always fair," he replied. "But those are the rules. If you don't like it, you can go back to Blue Rill Day Camp."

Julie and Ethan looked at each other, knowing they had little choice but to agree.

The rest of the meal proceeded uneventfully, with Maggie asking for a second helping of lasagna before devouring a large slice of Mrs. Danvers's cheesecake.

As Ethan followed her to the front door, he couldn't help □attempting to set up their next date. "If you're bored tomorrow, you can come over and we can finish that level," he suggested.

Maggie smiled at him on her way outside. "Sure. That sounds great. I'll let you know."

Back in the dining room, Julie made her exit during Maggie's goodbyes and snuck off to her room, leaving the adults alone for a moment.

Still thinking about the orphanage, a nagging feeling lingered in the back of Mrs. Danvers's mind that she couldn't shake. "Do you think someone could be living there?" she asked.

"Living where?" replied Mr. Danvers, his thoughts having already moved on to other topics.

"In the orphanage," she replied, wondering how he could have forgotten the previous conversation so quickly.

"Oh, right. I doubt it. They have that place sealed up tight, but I guess you never know."

"Well, don't you think someone should look into it? It's going to bother me, especially with the kids unattended for the summer."

"If it will make you feel better, I'll stop by the police station on my way to the office tomorrow morning," he offered. "I'll ask them to check it out."

"Thank you," she said. "It would. You know how nervous I get with the kids on their own all day. Knowing the sheriff will check on the building would really put my mind at ease."

By the time the sun went down, Gene Bell and Sheriff Bruce Cahill had finished the case of beer next to Gene's mini-fridge. The baseball field down the road sat empty, the children having all long gone home. Bruce, who failed to notify his wife of his after-hours detour, should have left hours ago as well. If he left now, she would smell the booze on him, which would inevitably lead to an argument, so he decided to keep Gene company a while longer.

"Oh, I almost forgot," Gene began, slurring his words. "I been meanin' to stop by the station and tell ya. I saw Eliza Wilkins snoopin' around the woods by the orphanage again last week."

"Oh yeah?" Bruce asked. "What was she doin?"

"Couldn't tell ya, but if you ask me, it looked like she was up to no good."

"Thanks for the report," he replied, attempting to sound sincere.

Bruce knew pushing back on Gene's accusations was pointless. After Gene had a few drinks in his system, the topic of conversation always turned to his daughters and eventually to accusations against Eliza. Bruce couldn't imagine what it would be like to lose his one child let alone losing two in the same night. He felt a sense of pity every time he looked at the man. He felt partially to blame for the family's lack of closure, but he had done everything in his power to find those girls. As far as he was concerned, they had dropped off the face of the Earth.

Like Gene, he suspected the Wilkins boy was involved with the disappearances, but with the boy missing too and zero evidence of a crime, his hands were tied. Every search turned up nothing, and eventually, the department had to move on to other matters.

"Have ya made any progress on gettin' another warrant to search that ole' witch's house?" Gene asked.

"Gene, we've been through this a thousand times. We searched her house when yer girls went missing. I'm the one who took the heat when nothin' turned up. You know she filed a harassment complaint with the district. I think she's hiding something too, but if we didn't find anythin' then, what makes ya think we'll find somethin' now? It's been almost fifteen years with no sign of the girls or her son."

"I just know it. I feel it in my bones," he replied. "We can catch her off guard. I wouldn't be surprised if she killed them all, her own son included!"

Bruce rolled his eyes. "Gene, you have *got* to cool it with the conspiracy theories. You're lucky it's just me here. If that got back to her, she could sue you for libel."

"You think I give a shit about that? She can't take what I don't have," he replied. "What about those dogs? You know the dead-body sniffing ones? We didn't have those back when the girls went missing, but I'll bet you could bring in one real easy nowadays."

The sheriff considered Gene's suggestion. It actually wasn't that bad of an idea. "Yer right, but the fact of the matter is the court just won't agree to another search warrant without any new evidence. I'm sorry, but it's just the way it is. I know it's tough to hear, but you really just need to consider moving on."

"Fuck that!" Gene yelled, slamming his hands down on the workbench. "Would you just move on if it were your kid?"

"Listen, Gene, I don't mean that. It's just that this obsession isn't doing your mental or physical health any favors."

"Yeah, whatever," Gene replied, eyeing his gun rack. "One of these days I'm gonna do the entire town a favor and get rid of her for good."

Bruce shook his head in disbelief. "I don't know what that's supposed to mean," he said. "But you can't go around saying that kinda stuff, especially to the sheriff. You're lucky I've had a few and am very off-duty right now, but you've got to cool it."

Gene didn't like anyone telling him how to speak, especially inside his home. As far as he was concerned, if anything happened to Eliza Wilkins, she had it coming.

With the mood soured, the sheriff made his exit, returning home in his cruiser with no regard for his blood alcohol level. He made sure to give Gene one more reminder to cool his temper on his way out the door.

Fairfield Gazzette

Early Edition   Fairfield's First Choice for News Since 1926   Vol. 32 No. 10

50¢

September 2, 1980

STATE LAUNCHES INVESTIGATION INTO FAIRFIELD CHILDREN'S HOME

The State Department of Child Welfare has opened a formal investigation into the Fairfield Children's Home after discovering a number of missing and possibly falsified adoption records.

Officials confirmed that at least four case files contained inconsistent documentation and signatures that did not match parental records on file. Several children listed as "relocated" have yet to be accounted for.

When contacted by the Gazette, Headmaster Patrick Brennan insisted the discrepancies were the result of a clerical error and accused state inspectors of political grandstanding.

"Every child in my care is safe and well," Brennan said. "We have nothing to hide."

Investigators are expected to return to the facility later this week to conduct interviews with staff and residents. A spokesperson for the Department described the situation as deeply troubling but declined to comment further until the audit is complete.

CHAPTER 7

The sun had just risen, slicing through the lingering layer of fog that coated Fairfield on a lazy Saturday morning. Most of the neighborhood was still in bed when a pair of bikes came barreling down the street, kicking up dust in their wake. The bicycles veered off the pavement, hopping the curb as they did so, and came to a stop in front of a yellow house.

Connor and Noah dumped their bikes on the well-manicured lawn and ran up to the door. Connor pressed the doorbell repeatedly while Noah called out at the top of his lungs. "Maggie! Get out here!" he yelled, his voice echoing down the street.

The boys gave no thought to the early hour on Saturday and that neighbors may still have been asleep. After a minute of hollering, the front door creaked open and Maggie stuck her head out, her hair still a mess of tangles from just rolling out of bed.

"Hey, guys. What are you doing here so early?" she asked.

"We're headed down to the trails, probably check out the lake for some swimming later. Put on some clothes and let's go," explained Connor.

"Oh, that sounds fun," Maggie replied. "But I was thinking about going over to Ethan's in a bit to play some video games."

"That sounds more like a punishment," said Noah with a laugh. "It's the first full day of summer vacation. Look at the weather. It's going to be a perfect day."

Maggie shielded her eyes and glanced up at the sky. He was right. Even at that early hour, the sun had already warmed the air, causing shimmering waves of steam to rise from the ground.

She hesitated a moment longer as she weighed her promise to Ethan against a day with Noah and Connor at the lake. Ethan wouldn't be happy if she ditched him, but she didn't want to sit inside on such a beautiful day, either. There was no way Noah and Connor would let her invite him along, so she saw no point in asking. She didn't understand why boys had to be so mean to each other. Finally, she gave in, running back inside the house to throw on a pair of shorts before hopping on her bike and falling into step between her two friends.

Across the street, Ethan sat up in bed, woken up by the noise outside his window. Stealthily, he peered through the blinds to see who was causing the ruckus. His heart sank when he spotted Connor and Noah on the front porch of Maggie's house. He watched her emerge while the boys spoke animatedly. They shared a laugh, and after a minute, she disappeared into her house.

For a moment, his spirits lifted, thinking she had turned the boys away. But instead of leaving, they waited on her stoop, and eventually, the garage door opened. Maggie returned wearing a new outfit, rolling her bike into the driveway. A pang of disappointment settled in his chest. He had been hoping she would come over to finish the game they were playing. He had everything set up. The controllers were all charged, snacks planned, and he had a new playlist of songs he had curated specifically for her. But it seemed like he would be spending the day alone.

He slumped back in bed, punching the side of his pillow as he did. Why did Noah and Connor always have to swoop in and ruin everything? And why did Maggie seem to like hanging out with them so much?

Down below, Maggie glanced up at Ethan's room as they pedaled away. She thought she saw his blinds move slightly, although it could have been the sun's reflection in her eye.

Connor noticed her sideways glance, and with a shrewd grin on his face, he asked, "So, what's the deal with you and Ethan?" His tone remained casual but his words pointed.

Maggie scrunched her face at the question. "What do you mean?"

Noah snickered. "Yeah, like, why do you hang out with him? He's kinda weird."

"And boring," Connor added. "All he does is stay inside and sulk."

Maggie tensed up, her grip tightening on her handlebars. "He's not boring," she said firmly. "Ethan's cool. He's just... quiet. You guys don't even know him."

Noah rolled his eyes. "We know enough. He's in half of our classes. He's always so moody. It's like he thinks he's better than everyone."

"That's not true. He's nice. Nicer than you. I bet he wouldn't threaten to punch someone over a baseball game," Maggie shot back.

"Yeah, well, maybe I should have knocked his lights out," Noah replied. "That little shit got lucky."

"Real manly, resorting to violence when you lose," Maggie said. "You don't have to like him, but that doesn't give you the right to trash him, either."

The boys exchanged a look but didn't press the issue further, though Connor couldn't resist muttering, "Whatever. He's still weird."

The trio turned off the road and onto a narrow dirt trail. Popular with nature enthusiasts and the quickest route to the lake, the well-worn trail wound its way through the trees behind a row of houses.

A town parks department sign hung at the entryway to the hiking trail, listing the rules for use of the path.

They had barely gone a few yards when a figure stepped out from behind a cluster of trees, startling them. The three slammed on their brakes and skidded to a stop in front of a woman.

The town outcast, Eliza Wilkins, blocked their path, her long, dark dress billowing in the breeze. She eyed the kids with a mix of hesitation and concern, her gaze fixing on each of them in turn. "You three need to stay away from the orphanage," she said, her voice firm. "It's not safe. You don't know what's in there."

Noah snorted, clearly unimpressed. "Like what, ghosts?" he asked mockingly.

"Or the boogeyman?" added Connor, not wanting to be left out of the fun.

Eliza didn't flinch. "This is not a time for jokes. Keep your distance. That building is no place for children."

Noah smirked, nudging Connor with his elbow. "Maybe she thinks a pedophile is gonna snatch us up."

"Maybe it's you we should be afraid of," said Connor. "I heard you grind up human bones for your potions."

Maggie frowned, noticing Eliza's despondent reaction to the quips. Inspecting her with a mix of curiosity and unease, she asked, "Why? What's so dangerous about it, anyway? It's been abandoned for years. No one goes up there."

Eliza pressed her lips together. "Heed my warning," she said. "And tell your friends. Something is coming. Something bad."

With that, she turned and walked away, disappearing back into the trees as swiftly as she had appeared. For a moment, the kids were silent, her words of warning lingering in their minds.

Then Noah burst out laughing. "Man, she's nuts. Did you see the way she was looking at us? Like we're about to get murdered or something."

Connor chuckled, shaking his head. "Yeah, she's crazy. Doesn't she realize those kids went missing ages ago? The place has been empty forever. Total loony tunes."

Maggie didn't join her friends in laughing. She looked back in the direction Eliza went, her brow furrowed.

Something about the encounter didn't sit right with her, but she kept her thoughts to herself. Instead, she followed the boys as they rode deeper into the woods, her mind turning over Eliza's warning.

CHAPTER 8

Ethan Danvers stared out his bedroom window long after watching Noah, Connor, and Maggie disappear around the curve of the road. He balled up his fists in anger, thinking about them spending the day together. He didn't understand what she saw in them. Those knuckleheads would probably end up stuck in this podunk town their entire existence, while Ethan wanted to do something with his life. He couldn't wait to move away to college and never look back. He just had to make it through the next five years with those jerks taunting him at every corner.

At least in the meantime he had the fantasy worlds of his games to keep his mind occupied. Thinking about his game, he hopped out of bed, knowing the sooner he started playing, the sooner he would forget being ditched by Maggie. After scarfing down a bowl of cereal, he grabbed his lucky controller and booted up the console. He selected his new game, *Undead Uprising 4,* but instead of continuing where they left off the previous day, he started a new game in hopes Maggie would eventually return to continue.

He blasted a few of the undead running toward him but couldn't concentrate. Within seconds, he found himself overwhelmed. A swarm of the creatures closed in on him, and a blood-spattered message letting him know he died appeared on the screen. He reloaded the game, but the horde immediately tore him apart again. His head just wasn't into it. Frustrated, he turned the game off and tossed the controller onto his bed. How could he focus on the game knowing Maggie was off doing who knew what with Noah and Connor?

Unable to enjoy his favorite pastime, he lay back down, frustrated at the disappointing start to his summer. Staring at his ceiling, Ethan's mind raced. Part of him had the urge to go out on his bike and find out what Noah, Connor, and Maggie were up to. Although they were already well ahead of him, he had a pretty good idea where they were headed. But the thought of getting caught spying on them was too big of a risk.

Instead, another idea crossed his mind—something that had been itching at him since the previous day. He knew one surefire way to impress Maggie and show those idiots he wasn't such a pussy after all. He just needed to get out of the house without his sister tagging along. If he was quick, he could be gone before she noticed.

He put on his favorite pair of jeans, along with a red T-shirt emblazoned with the Flash logo, and headed down the stairs. He paused after hearing movement in the kitchen, but it was only his mother preparing herself something to eat.

She saw Ethan come down and greeted him. "Dressed already?" she asked. "Are you hungry?"

"No, Mom. I'm headed across the street to Maggie's for a little while. I'll be back in a few hours."

"Oh, okay," she replied with a smile. "Glad to see you two hanging out together again."

Ethan threw on his shoes and ran out the door without another word. He waited a moment to make sure his mother didn't look out the window after him and grabbed his bike from the driveway. If all went as planned, he would be back before anyone noticed it missing.

It only took a few minutes to reach his destination. He pulled to a stop along the locked gate leading to the orphanage. He set his bike down and looked up at the fence surrounding the property. It was taller than he remembered. Climbing it would be easy enough, but the spiked points at the top concerned him. He could likely get by them unscathed, but one wrong move could spell disaster. If he got hurt, there wasn't anyone around to help. Suddenly, he wondered if this was such a good idea after all.

Before attempting to scale the fence, something told him to scout the perimeter in search of another way in that didn't involve risking his limbs. After turning the corner, he found exactly what he was looking for. One section of the fence was detached from the others, leaning away from the rest. With all the hoopla surrounding the building, he was surprised the maintenance crews had allowed it to fall into such disrepair. He figured they had gotten lazy with just about everything in town.

Ethan grasped the old iron post and pulled on the leaning bar, hoping to widen the opening before attempting to squeeze through. The fence moved, but only slightly. He was lucky he didn't have much meat on his bones. He inhaled deeply, sucking in his belly as he maneuvered through the gap, shoulder first. A second later, he was officially trespassing.

Growing up, the fence had seemed like an impenetrable barrier that held back the evil forces of hell. Finally standing on the other side was a bit anticlimactic. He didn't feel any different. He thought it was funny that the fear of something was usually scarier than the □thing itself.

Not wanting to spend any more time inside the orphanage than absolutely necessary, he headed up the hill toward the main building. He followed the remnants of an overgrown path leading to the front door. When he reached the door and looked up, he suddenly realized how large the building was. Finding the ball he hit might not be as easy as running in, grabbing it, and running out again. He considered turning around, but he had already gone that far, and if he chickened out, that would just prove Noah right.

He took a step back to examine the building and determine the general direction of the window where the ball landed. Like everything on the property, the old structure had been reclaimed by nature. Ivy clung to the siding, twisting outward in every direction. Small purple flowers bloomed from the vines. Ethan's gaze followed the row of flowers up to the window as if he was following a breadcrumb trail of petals.

The window stood open, just as he remembered from the day before. He understood why his father doubted his story, but seeing the open window solidified his commitment to going inside to find the ball. Based on the position of the window, the room should be on the west side of the second floor. He didn't think it would be hard to find but remembered getting inside the building might not be as easy as squeezing between the fence posts. Before searching for a way in, he checked the doorknob, and to his surprise, it opened right up. Between the open window and the unlocked front door, he wondered if some older kids had been using the building as a hangout spot to drink beer or get high. He never considered the possibility that the door might have been left unlocked especially for him.

The rusty hinges of the old wooden door screamed as he pushed it open, as if warning him to stay away. The piercing sound echoed through the empty halls. Before stepping inside, a wave of warm air hit his face as it rushed to escape the orphanage's grasp. The place smelled of mildew and decay, mingled with something else—a strange, sweet scent, like overripe fruit. Beams of sunlight burst through the open door, illuminating patches of the dark foyer, but it was the unusual vegetation that caught his attention. A thick, furry moss marbled with shades of blue and purple covered the walls. Vines unlike any he had ever seen stretched along the floor and slithered up the walls. The creeping plants formed a network of stems, leaves, and tendrils that ran throughout the house. The vines seemed to breathe on their own, pulsing in rhythm with his heart, which he suddenly realized was racing.

He took a deep breath to calm his nerves. *Some overgrown plants can't hurt me*, he thought. "Hello?" he whispered, not loud enough for anyone to hear. "Grab the ball and get out," he muttered, taking a step inside.

The air was hot and humid. He wiped his forehead with his shirt, catching a bead of sweat that ran down his cheek. He walked deeper into the orphanage, following his memory of the baseball's trajectory. If he could find the stairs, he would be up and out in no time.

But the room dimmed with each step he took. Any light that found its way in from the entrance or cracks in the boarded-up windows was quickly lost in the dark expanse of the large building. With the sun bright in the sky, bringing a flashlight never crossed Ethan's mind. He proceeded slowly, giving his eyes time to adjust to the darkness. Finally, his vision sharpened, and he found what he was looking for. A large set of stairs curved up and around at the rear of the main hallway. They, like everything else in sight, were covered in the creeping vines. He looked up hesitantly at the dark hall above and swallowed.

Instinctively, he put his hand on the banister but jerked it away when he felt something squirm under his palm. The unsettling feeling caused a tingling sensation of goosebumps to run down his back. "You've got this," he whispered, forcing himself to continue his ascent. As he climbed the stairs, he became increasingly aware of the plants. They seemed to curl and shift as he passed. He swore he saw a vine retract as his foot landed near it, but when he stopped for a closer look, it was still. He gritted his teeth and stepped lightly as he quickened his pace up the steps.

By the time he reached the top of the stairs, he expected to be in almost total darkness. The thought of having to rely on his hands to blindly feel his way around terrified him, but when he reached the top, a strange glow emanated throughout the hall as if the house itself was giving off light.

Thankful for the illumination, he didn't dwell on its source and continued on. Shifting his weight from the top step to the hallway, he cringed when the floorboards groaned beneath him. He took a deep breath and reminded himself that he was alone in the building, so he had nothing to fear.

He navigated the corridor carefully, stepping deliberately to avoid the plants covering much of the rotting floor. Eventually, he came to a room with the door slightly ajar. A single beam of natural light escaped from the opening. He pushed the door open farther and peered inside. He spotted the open window, confirming he found the correct room.

He stepped inside, scanning the warped wooden floor, but didn't see the ball. Frowning, Ethan crouched and peered under an old desk. Nothing. He kicked at a few vines, wondering if they concealed the ball, but still couldn't find it. His stomach twisted. He knew it should be there.

Just as he turned to leave, a faint sound caught his ear, and he spun around just in time to see something appear from the shadows. The baseball rolled from the corner as if it had been pushed. It slowed to a stop in the center of the room amid a tangle of roots, their tendrils glowing faintly with a soft, spectral blue.

A sense of relief came over him upon seeing the ball, and he bent down to pick it up. But his relief was short-lived when he heard a faint chittering from the shadows. He froze, heart pounding, and looked in the direction of the sound.

In the corner of the room, hidden by the plants and darkness, something stirred. Ethan squinted, trying to make out the shape, but when he thought he saw a form, it shifted and was lost in the shadows.

"W-who's there?" he called.

He should have turned and run, but something drew him closer. He inched forward, his feet shuffling along the floor until he saw a pale shape hunched in the corner; he was certain of it. Almost as if waiting for Ethan's acceptance of its existence, the figure emerged from the shadow. It was a child, or something like one.

The creature was his size, maybe even his shape, but its features could barely pass for human. The color of its skin was bone white. Abnormally large, yellow eyes gleamed, reflecting a ray of light from the window. Colorless, long, wispy hair reached below its bony shoulders. Its limbs were long and thin, and when it moved, it did so in a way that looked unnatural, as if it had only recently learned to use its body.

Ethan stumbled back. "S-stay away."

The creature stepped forward, mimicking his movements.

Ethan's heart pounded. He lifted a hand, palm out, to keep it back, but couldn't prevent his arm from shaking. Across the room, the thing lifted its own hand in the same manner.

Suddenly, Ethan felt a sharp pain in his calf. He looked down to see that the roots were wound around his legs and were burrowing into his flesh. He twisted his legs in an attempt to free them but was unable to gain any leverage against the coiling plants. "No," Ethan said as he struggled against the roots.

The creature's mouth moved, its lips forming an O, but no sound came out. Then, slowly, its voice cracked in a raspy, high-pitched tone. "No," it echoed.

Ethan's throat closed. He shook his head violently, and the creature copied. It crept forward awkwardly, its jerky movements silent on the warped boards.

"Go away!" Ethan shouted.

"Go away," the thing repeated, its grin widening until a trickle of black fluid dribbled down its chin. Though the creature was horrific in some ways, it was strangely beautiful in others. Its soft features evoked a feeling of familiarity that eased the boy's fear.

As it neared him, Ethan's legs buckled, but the roots kept him upright. He lifted his arm to shield himself, and the creature reached out in return, pressing its palm against his. The touch was gentle yet jarring. An icy sensation burned at the point of contact and slowly worked its way up his arm.

He wanted to pull away, but he couldn't. He tried to inhale, but his lungs refused to cooperate. His stomach clenched. The orphanage spun around him, tilting at odd angles. He needed to go home. The dimly lit room grew even darker, and his limbs grew numb. He looked at his arms held out in front of him and saw the color draining before his eyes. Something wasn't right. He tried again to wrestle himself free, but his efforts were futile.

Meanwhile, something was happening to the creature. A series of loud cracks splintered through the air as its bones fractured and reformed. The pale-white color of its skin darkened, and its facial features changed. Sunken cheekbones filled out, and soft features solidified, morphing to match Ethan's own until he felt like he was looking in a mirror. But if he looked in a real mirror, he would've seen his complexion fade to an unhealthy gray, his skin shriveling as the creature pulled itself closer to him.

"Ethan," the creature whispered. The voice coming out of its mouth was almost perfect in tone. It sounded just like him.

The world lurched sideways, and Ethan's vision darkened. The last thing he felt was the creature's cold breath against his ear, whispering his own voice back to him as everything went black and the roots consumed him.

CHAPTER 9

The thing that looked like Ethan crouched over the boy's twitching body, maintaining contact with the child while the process completed. Their pale skin had darkened, becoming warm with color. Their bones shifted, shortening in places and expanding in others. Their spine stretched and popped with wet cracks as it reshaped. The thin, wispy hair on top of their head darkened until it matched the light brown of Ethan's locks. Their shoulders narrowed, legs thickened, and jaw reformed.

The metamorphosis continued until every aspect of the creature had changed, molding them into the familiar form of a thirteen-year-old boy. The process was painful for the creature. With each crack of bone and tear of tendon, they let out a stifled cry as they fantasized of the opportunities their new form would enjoy.

They took a breath, then another. They flexed their fingers and turned their head from side to side, testing the movement and weight of their new body. They examined their genitals with curiosity. Though the transformation was painful, the metamorphosis was essential to complete their life cycle.

They trembled, holding their skull in both hands as a torrent of memories rushed in: Ethan as a child, growing up with his sister Julie, Maggie's laugh, and the smell of lasagna from last night's dinner. Every sight and sound from thirteen years of living flooded into their mind. The creature swayed but did not fall. Finally, the rush of memories slowed, and they staggered upright, flexing their shoulders as they straightened their posture.

Ethan's body lay still in the center of the derelict room. His eyes were open, fixed on the sagging ceiling above, but they were hollow inside. His face had lost its color, and his skin had shriveled as if he had been swimming far too long.

The thing that killed Ethan stood over the corpse and watched in silence. They took no pleasure in the life they took but felt no remorse for snuffing out the young soul.

As the creature backed away, the vines closed in. They slid up from the cracked floorboards and out from the shadowed corners like serpents searching for their next meal. Thin tendrils probed Ethan's skin, wrapping around his wrists and ankles and sliding underneath his clothes.

The roots secreted a dark liquid as they explored the child, beginning the digestion process. The first puncture was small, a vine burrowing into the indentation of his belly button, while another made its way into his anus. A wet sound followed as more dug into his ears and nostrils. Ethan's skin sank inward, his body deflating like a punctured balloon.

The vines pulsed as they drank, swelling with the stolen fluids. Muscles shriveled and bones cracked as his form gave way. His face withered and his cheeks sank into his skull while his lips peeled back, exposing his graying gums. The boy's hazel eyes dimmed to a cloudy film before they collapsed into sludge.

The stench of decay filled the room, but it was accelerated and unnatural. Years of decomposition compressed into minutes. What was once Ethan sagged into a dark slurry, soaking the wood beneath him until only a faint black stain remained.

Then the boy who was not Ethan crouched over the spot where the child had been, sniffing the air. The last vines slid away into the floor, leaving no trace of what they devoured save a set of flattened clothes. They collected the garments and dressed themselves. The creature, indistinguishable from the boy they replaced, picked up the scuffed baseball from the floor. They inspected it for a moment before placing the ball in their pocket and emerging into an unfamiliar human world.

Maggie only ▯stayed at the lake with Noah and Connor for a short while. Although she was having fun, she felt guilty for ditching Ethan. She understood why he disliked the other boys so much. They were complete dicks to him, but they acted differently when he wasn't around. She figured stopping over to see if he was still up for a gaming session was the least she could do.

After arriving home, she took a quick shower to clean off the dried pond scum, then headed across the street. She rang the doorbell, and was greeted by a confused Mrs. Danvers.

"Hello, Mrs. Danvers. I was wondering if Ethan was around?" she asked.

"Hi, Maggie," his mother replied. "I don't think he's home. He left a while ago and told me he was going to your house."

"My house? I just got back from the lake."

Mrs. Danvers's expression changed from confused to concerned at the revelation Ethan had lied to her.

Seeing this, Maggie hesitated. She hadn't meant to get Ethan in trouble, but she had no way of knowing he had used her as an excuse to get out of the house. Although she hadn't meant to blow up his spot, she didn't appreciate being used as a cover story without a heads up of the situation.

Mrs. Danvers turned away and took a step back into the house, calling for Ethan as she walked toward the stairs. She considered he may have returned without her noticing, but when she checked his room to find it empty, her frustration with the boy increased.

Hearing the commotion, Ethan's father joined in the search and promptly noticed the missing bike.

"Where would he have gone?" Mrs. Danvers asked, her anger turning back to panic. "Should we go looking for him?"

"Relax," Mr. Danvers replied. "He's a kid on summer vacation. I'm sure he's fine."

"But he never goes anywhere. And what reason would he have to lie?"

"I'm not sure why he lied, but we'll deal with that when he gets back."

As if on cue, a cloud of dust appeared at the end of the road, where a small figure on a bike at the center of the plume rode toward the house. The group stopped their conversation and watched in anticipation as Ethan pulled into the driveway. He set his bike in its usual spot on the side of the house and joined the others.

His parents stood on the stoop, staring at him, waiting for an explanation, yet he remained silent.

"Well?" Mrs. Danvers asked impatiently. "Where have you been?"

"Hi, Mom. I was riding my bike," he replied matter-of-factly. "I'm home now."

"We can see that you're home," his father said. "You told your mother you were going to Maggie's house, yet that was clearly not the case. Got anything to say for yourself?"

For a split second, something flickered in his eyes and it looked like he was about to speak, but then he stopped, his face returning to a blank expression. "Sorry," he said sheepishly. "I guess I got mixed up."

"Mixed up?" his mother replied. "Ethan, that's not like you. You know better than to lie to me. And what happened to your clothes? They're filthy."

Ethan just stared at her, offering no reply. The entire situation became so awkward Maggie considered silently backing away from the house and letting them deal with their family drama on their own.

"Well, you're grounded," Mrs. Danvers said, breaking the silence. "No video games. No going out."

Maggie winced at the dreaded words. She hadn't meant to get him in trouble. He was going to be furious with her. She glanced at him, waiting for his forthcoming reaction. She expected him to protest, to argue that it wasn't a big deal.

Instead, Ethan just nodded. "Okay."

Mrs. Danvers studied him for a long moment before sighing. "Go to your room. We'll talk later."

Ethan obeyed without hesitation, brushing past Maggie without another word. She watched him go, unease creeping up her spine. Ethan loved video games. He would've fought tooth and nail to keep them. But for some reason, he didn't even seem to care.

Something strange was going on. Her mind wandered back to the cause of the argument. Where had Ethan gone? And what reason did he have to lie to his parents about it?

Eliza Wilkins moved carefully along the perimeter of the orphanage, the smudge stick in her hand trailing a line of fragrant smoke behind her. The last remnants of sunlight were shrinking through the overgrown trees, but she needed no light to complete her task. She had performed the same ritual countless times before.

She murmured under her breath, words of protection that she recited from memory as she traced the same path Ethan took only a few hours before. Unaware of the boy's visit to the orphanage, an ominous feeling gnawed at her as she circled the building.

Then she saw it.

A section of the iron fence had broken away from the rest. Immediately, she noticed the twisted metal hinges and unnaturally deformed posts. Nearby, the ground was disturbed. She bent over to sift through a pile of rusted screws that lay in the grass. They, too, were misshapen as if they had forced their way out.

A knot formed in her throat. Something had escaped. She knew, without a doubt, what it was—the same thing that took her Billy all those years ago.

A chill ran through her bones, and she pressed her palm against the cold iron, whispering another incantation. It wasn't enough. Not anymore. She had grown complacent. And something was loose in Fairfield once again.

 Chapter 10

G ene Bell sat alone at his kitchen table, a half-empty beer can sweating against the wooden surface. The house was quiet. It had been ever since Liz and Sarah went missing. No laughter. No sibling arguments. No footsteps running down the hall. The silence was deafening. He took a slow sip of his beer, barely registering his actions as he swallowed each gulp of the beverage. His thoughts fixated on the sheriff's words as they echoed inside his head.

We did everything we could, Gene.

Bullshit. If they had done everything they could, they would have found his girls, or at least figured out what happened to them. They would still be out there looking and wouldn't have stopped until they had answers. With no trace of the girls and not even a proper burial, he couldn't move on. Everyone expected him to just let it go. He couldn't do that no matter how many years it had been. He wouldn't.

He stood up and walked over to the framed photograph of the twins he kept on the counter. It was the same picture that had been plastered all over missing persons flyers and news reports for months following their disappearance. But like everything else in this high-speed world, attention soon shifted to the next big story, and his girls were forgotten. His daughters' faces smiled back from the faded photo, their bright eyes filled with life that had been taken too soon.

Gene exhaled sharply, rubbing a hand over his face. His fingers curled into a fist as his sorrow turned into rage. No one would ever find them. Hell, everyone else had stopped looking. The sheriff stopped caring years ago. It was up to Gene. Someone had to pay for what happened to his girls.

He set the frame down, replacing it with the shotgun from his rack. After checking the chamber, he grabbed his truck keys from their hook and headed out the door.

The dashboard of Gene's pickup rattled as it rolled down the road toward Eliza Wilkins's house. If anyone had answers, it was her. The way Gene saw it, her feigned ignorance only made her look guilty. He wasn't gullible enough to fall for her lies. If he had to guess, Eliza was probably the last person to see any of the missing kids alive, her son included. With the years slipping away, he had nothing left to lose and no intention of letting her take the truth to her grave. If anything, he regretted not acting sooner. He didn't know what he planned to do when he found her, but he couldn't sit back and do nothing any longer.

Dusk had settled by then. Gene turned off his headlights before reaching Eliza's house in an attempt to avoid drawing attention, but he couldn't do anything about the loud rumble of his pickup's engine. He put his truck in park and watched the house for a moment. No lights, no movement inside. It didn't even look like she was home. Just his luck.

He considered turning off his engine and waiting for her to show up but spotted her car parked in the driveway and realized she couldn't have gone far. His jaw tightened. If she wasn't home, there was only one other place she could be. He threw the truck into gear, rigidly gripping the steering wheel in a mix of anger and frustration.

The orphanage loomed in the distance, its dark outline growing more pronounced against the early evening sky. Even if his girls went into Fairfield Manor and never came out, the building itself wasn't to blame for their deaths. And he didn't buy into Eliza's fairy tales, either. There was a human element involved and Eliza knew more than she let on. That alone made her just as responsible as her son.

Part of him didn't actually expect to find Eliza back at the scene of the crime, but as he approached the old building, he spotted a figure along the perimeter of the fence. The sight of her caused his lip to curl up in a snarl. There she was, caught in the act of performing some arcane ritual on the very site where his girls went missing. Who would do that except for the guilty party? The bundle of smoking weeds she waved in the air and her tongue's rapid movements as she whispered an unholy incantation told him everything he needed to know. He didn't have to hear her to know that the words she spoke weren't from any of the Lord's prayers. The police search of the building might have come up empty, but seeing Eliza creep along the fence confirmed his suspicions that she held the answer he was looking for.

Gene slowed the truck and pulled onto the shoulder, watching as she moved along the perimeter. His stomach turned at the sight of her witchcraft. Smoke curled up around her, carrying a strange scent through the air. She supposedly lost her son too, but that wasn't grief. That wasn't mourning. It was something else. He didn't know what she was doing, but he couldn't let it continue.

Gene slammed the door as he stepped out of the truck, his boots crunching against the gravel. "What the hell do you think you're doing?" he yelled.

She didn't look up.

Clenching his fists, he called her name. "Eliza!"

Finally, she turned to face him, her eyes squinting with displeasure at his presence. Her fingers trembled around the smoldering bundle of herbs in her clutches. "You shouldn't be here," she said.

"*I* shouldn't be here?" he spat. "How about we start with what you're doing creeping around this place in the middle of the goddamn night."

Eliza took a step closer, her expression frantic. "You don't understand," she said, motioning toward the property. "I spent fifteen years trying to keep the barrier intact, but it was all for naught. The seal is broken. It has escaped."

Gene narrowed his eyes. "What's escaped? What are you talking about?"

"It hides among the children," she said, her voice pleading for belief. "They're in danger."

His blood ran cold and his mind went back to his daughters. He grabbed her by the arm. "What did you do?"

Eliza gasped as she twisted in an attempt to free herself from Gene's grasp. "Let go of me," she yelled.

"*Did you take them?*" His voice broke. "Did Billy take them? You lied for him. What are you hiding?"

Eliza ignored the accusations. "You're not listening to me," she exclaimed. "Something has escaped! The same thing that took my Billy. The same thing that took your girls."

The mere mention of his daughters from that witch's tongue sent Gene into a blind rage. He yanked her arm forward, causing her to lose her balance. He was tired of her games, her nonsense, her lies. Of course she would say whatever was necessary to protect her son.

Eliza suddenly lunged forward, catching Gene lost in his thoughts and off-guard. She pressed the smoking bundle of herbs against his forearm. The smudge stick burned straight through his flesh, filling the air with the acrid scent of burned hair and charred skin.

Gene let out a roar, releasing his grip on Eliza and stumbling backward as the searing pain shot up his arm.

"You stubborn fool," she hissed, backing away. "I'm not your enemy. I'm the only one who can stop it. But I fear we are too late." Before Gene had a chance to recover from the injury, she turned and bolted into the woods, disappearing in the shadows.

Gene clutched his arm, the pain making his vision blur. He considered going after her but hesitated. She knew those woods better than him. He would never catch up to her in the darkness.

His breath was ragged as he turned toward the orphanage one last time, half expecting to see something watching from the old building. But it stood the same as always, just an empty, rotting building and the faint scent of burning sage lingering in the night air.

He spat on the ground and climbed back into his truck, his burn throbbing with every movement as it began to blister. The pain only added fuel to the rage smoldering inside him. He would find that bitch and force her tell him the truth about what happened to his daughters, no matter what it took. And then he would make damn sure she paid for her role in their disappearance.

Fairfield Gazzette

Early Edition   Fairfield's First Choice for News Since 1926   Vol. 32 No. 10

November 3, 1981

FAIRFIELD HOME CLOSED AMID CHILD TRAFFICKING ALLEGATIONS

The Fairfield Children's Home was permanently closed this week following shocking allegations that children in the institution's care were illegally transferred and sold to private parties across state lines, bypassing official oversight.

A joint task force from the State Department of Child Welfare and Fairfield County Sheriff's Office confirmed evidence of falsified adoption papers, destroyed ledgers, and unaccounted for children.

Headmaster Patrick Brennan, who operated the Home since its founding in 1975, denied any involvement and blamed it on nothing more than sloppy record keeping. The headmaster maintains that no children have gone missing from his facility. "My life's work has been ruined because of lies," he told reporters as officials escorted him from the premises.

Mayor Harold Jenkins called the revelations "a stain on our town's conscience," vowing full cooperation with state authorities.

The building has been sealed pending further investigation. Former residents are being relocated while authorities search for additional victims.

CHAPTER II

The next morning, Finley Faywin awoke in a strange bed and a strange body, afraid to open their eyes and confirm what they already knew. Finley wished it was all a dream and they would find themselves back in the safety of their grove, but this was no dream. The lingering pain coursing through their body reminded them of the harsh reality of their recent transformation. They had an important job to do. The fate of their people was at stake.

Although they had studied diligently for the journey to the human world, training couldn't have prepared them for the agony they had undertaken. The metamorphosis took a toll on the body. Pain was to be expected. However, the pain didn't stop at Finley's skin or even the muscle underneath. The ache resonated deep in their bones. Thankfully, the discomfort would subside once their body settled into its new form.

Finley had been away from their refuge for less than a day, yet the ache of homesickness had already taken hold. They had no desire to leave their sanctuary and risk exposure to the humans. If anything went wrong, they were on their own. None of the elders would put themselves in peril for their sake. Most were too weak to survive long in the human realm, and the others would sooner seal the portal and remain hidden away than risk their own lives. But Finley wouldn't fail. Their task was too important. Too much was riding on their success to consider any other outcome. So they would do what was required of them, alone in an unfamiliar world.

Of all the peculiar sensations Finley encountered thus far, the odor emanating from the humans was the most unsettling. With each inhale, their strange scent permeated Finley's sinuses. They found it revolting that the disagreeable smell seeped from the humans' pores in the form of moisture secreted through the skin. Finley tasted the sickly sweet liquid on the back of their tongue. It reminded them of fruit that had soured in the sun. They didn't understand why they urinated the foul oil out of their pores rather than include it with their liquid waste. And after sleeping all night in the boy's bed, Finley reeked of the repulsive smell.

Eventually, they opened their eyes, blinking slowly as their pupils adjusted to their surroundings. The radiating pain left no organ untouched. The intense pressure squeezing Finley's eyeballs made them feel ready to burst at any moment. To make matters worse, the dry air of this world caused each blink to burn like sandpaper scraping against their corneas.

But through all their discomfort, the bed they lay on was the first human luxury that delighted them. The welcoming material of the mattress, paired with the fuzzy blanket wrapped around Finley's body, eased their pain. If it wasn't for the nagging responsibility of their mission, they could be content remaining in that bed for eternity.

Reluctantly, Finley rose to a sitting position and looked around the dwelling. Photographs and illustrations typical of a young boy's room plastered the walls. One featured a composite of humans and robots wielding various weapons, with a mechanical moon in the sky, while another featured an image of uniformed men and women, many wearing masks. The day before, Finley had been unfamiliar with any of the characters, but after absorbing the boy's memories, they could recite the original Star Wars trilogy line for line and knew the origin story of every member of the Justice League. That the humans wasted so much time and energy on such trivial things baffled them. The effort put into the productions would be better spent improving the lives of their people.

To Finley, the obsessions just reinforced what they had been taught their entire life. The humans' rapid geographical and technological advancements made the species lazy and weak. It diverted their focus away from what truly mattered. The traditions of the old ways were lost to them. But their willful blindness to the world's natural order was a blessing to Finley's kind as it allowed them to remain hidden over the centuries.

At one time long ago, the two species had lived in harmony together, but the humans' appetite for power and wealth had consumed them, and their destruction spread like a cancer, upsetting the Earth's natural order. Knowing the extent of the species' carelessness and greed lessened their guilt for their mission. They pitied the humans in the same manner a human might empathize with the cow on their dinner plate.

Finley placed their feet on the floor and stood, leaving the comfort and protection provided by the luxurious bed. The lush carpet fibers reminded Finley of walking in a field of velvety moss in the grove but without the annoyance of soiling their toes. Not that Finley minded the dirt, they lived their entire lives in it, after all, but Finley could grow to appreciate these human conveniences.

They reached the door and turned the knob, letting a sliver of light from the hallway illuminate the dark room. They put their ear to the opening and listened. Although they appeared human, their internal physiology remained unchanged. The inner workings of Finley's ear canal provided a wide range of hearing, allowing otherwise undetectable sounds to be heard crystal clear. Finley listened to the labored breathing of Ethan's father sitting at the kitchen table at the far end of the house. They heard the rustling newspaper as Mr. Danvers flipped the page and leaned over to take a sip of his morning coffee. The sizzling stove and wafting aroma enticed Finley, but they were not yet ready to mingle with the boy's family. The brief interaction the previous day had been terrifying enough.

Finley slunk out of Ethan's room and made their way to the bathroom down the hall. Once inside, within the relative safety of the locked door, Finley flicked the light switch and stood in front of the vanity. Looking in the mirror, they saw the face of a stranger staring back at them. Of course, the change was expected, but seeing another face in their reflection proved a jarring experience. They searched the boy in the mirror for a sign of recognition, maybe a familiar curve of the jaw or slope of the nose, but Finley noticed none of that. In awe of the completed transformation, Finley inspected themself closely as they practiced Ethan's facial expressions. They gazed deep into their own eyes, allowing the rest of their body to fall away from view. Although now a dull hazel instead of their natural yellow, when they looked past the corneas and deep into their pupils they saw the familiar spark that human souls lacked. Their true self remained. It was just hidden away from view.

Finley turned on the faucet and filled their hands with cold water, splashing it on their face. Another marvel of the human world. Finley had never seen running water before, save for the streams and creeks running through their land. The shocking cold grounded them, replacing their fear and trepidation with eagerness for the job. Their initial encounter went as well as could have been expected. Ethan's mother had been displeased with the boy, but she showed no sign of seeing through their guise. The child's punishment would allow Finley time to assimilate to their new body. Finley splashed another handful of water onto themselves, momentarily easing the pain coursing through them.

Dirty water rolled down Finley's cheeks and fell onto the rim of the sink, leaving brown stains that soiled the pristine white vanity. The soot reminded Finley they needed to be mindful of their odor. Just as the human smell was off-putting to them, their new companions would find Finley's scent peculiar as well. If not concealed, the aroma would bring suspicion upon them. But from what they had seen, even the humans disliked their own scent. Why else would they bathe so often and fill their shelves with perfumes, lotions, and sprays?

Finley undressed and turned on the shower, thankful for Ethan's memories. The information gained during the procedure was invaluable. Without his memories and knowledge of the human world, Finley would struggle to fit in. Mundane tasks such as turning on the shower would be difficult, while mimicking the boy well enough to fool his family would be near impossible.

They stepped into the shower, allowing the ice-cold water to engulf their body. Although their skin color had lost its beautiful pale tint, it retained the silky smooth texture it had always possessed. Finley was grateful that human adolescents bore finer hides than their elders. They doubted their complexion would ever recover if the transformation required imitating the coarse, wrinkled skin of an adult human. Not that their bones could undergo such a major reconstruction. The anatomy and similar size of the adolescent to Finley's kind made them ideal candidates for the substitution.

With their eyes closed and pain subdued, Finley's thoughts drifted. For a moment, they imagined they were back home, in their own skin. As their mind wandered, so did their hands, running up and down the length of their body, exploring its supple curves. Finley's new body varied in many ways from its natural form. Their hands lingered on their nipples, a foreign concept to them. They found it strange that human males grew teats but lacked the glands to produce milk. It was just another example of their inferior and inefficient anatomy.

Then they found another appendage that drew their interest—a bizarre looking protrusion jutting from between their legs. As his fingers found this strange organ, a warm sensation flowed through their chest. Finley took a deep breath as pleasure replaced their pain. They tilted their head back, letting the water flow down their chest and, for the first time, thought to themselves that their new form might have some advantages after all.

Suddenly, the doorknob jiggled and a loud bang interrupted Finley's private moment.

Ethan's sister's voice followed. "Hurry up in there. You're not the only one living in this house."

Startled, Finley turned off the shower, ending the soothing flow of water. They considered a response but froze. Convincing the humans they were Ethan was no simple task. One mistake could ruin everything.

With no reply, Julie called out through the locked door again. "Hello? Did you fall in the toilet?"

Finally, Finley replied. "Sorry. Just finishing up."

Julie hesitated before responding. "You sound weird. Are you feeling okay?"

Finley caught their breath. Did she know they were an imposter? "I'm still half asleep," they replied.

"I was thinking of riding to the field to see if anyone's hanging out," she said. "What do you think?"

"I'm not allowed out, remember? I think that means you're grounded too."

"Whatever. You know Dad will let us out if we promise to keep an eye on each other."

"I'm not feeling up to it today. I'll make it up to you tomorrow," said Finley, hoping the promise would placate Julie.

With a huff, she said, "Fine. Are you coming out soon, at least? I really gotta go."

"Just use Mom and Dad's bathroom and quit bugging me, okay?"

Finley heard Julie's footsteps trample away down the hall toward her parents' room. With the coast clear, they took their chance to exit the bathroom and return to the confines of Ethan's room. After years of preparation, there was no reason to rush. Once the agony of the transformation faded, they could focus fully on their mission.

CHAPTER 12

Finley remained hidden away in Ethan's room until the next morning, shooing away Ethan's parents when they came to check on him but thankful for the meals they delivered. Being grounded had its advantages, but Finley couldn't avoid their responsibilities forever. Luckily, the pain had already begun to lessen. So they sat stiffly at the breakfast table, forcing down mouthfuls of pancakes that tasted like inedible fungus. The warm, dense texture was unsettling and the taste overpowering in ways they hadn't expected. Food in the human world was richer and more complex but also strange. The flavors were pungent in some ways yet dull in others. They chewed methodically, mimicking what they had observed from Ethan's memories, but every bite was an effort.

They reached for the bottle of nectar and poured more syrup on the pancakes, drowning them in sugary goodness. Finley was thankful for the sweet topping.

They doubted they could choke down their meal without it.

Across the table, Julie was making her case.

"Come on, Dad," she whined, pleading for her brother's release from captivity. "Ethan's already been grounded for a whole day. Don't you think he's suffered enough?"

Mr. Danvers, engrossed in the newspaper, barely looked up. "He got himself grounded, Julie." He took a slow sip of coffee. "Actions have consequences."

"Yeah, but it's not like he killed anyone," she said, rolling her eyes. "We just want to hang out by the lake for a bit, or maybe at the ball field. Nothing crazy. You're always saying he needs to get out and socialize more."

Mr. and Mrs. Danvers gave each other a look. Julie was right. Most days they couldn't bribe Ethan to turn off his games and go outside. Maybe a reduced punishment would suffice. Ethan shouldn't have lied about going to Maggie's, but Julie had a point. His transgression was minor. Plus, Mr. Danvers didn't love the idea of her going down to the lake alone.

Finley felt everyone turn to them and realized too late that they had been sitting unnaturally still and quiet. Ethan would have been pleading his case along with his sister. They quickly adopted a hopeful expression and forced out a response. "I won't do anything stupid. Julie will keep an eye on me," they said, careful to match Ethan's tone. "Promise."

Mrs. Danvers frowned, studying them too closely for comfort. Finley focused their gaze on their plate, hoping she wouldn't notice anything amiss.

Mr. Danvers sighed. "Fine. But this doesn't mean the punishment is over. You're still not getting your video games back yet. And if you're late for dinner, you're grounded again. Both of you this time. No arguments."

Julie grinned in victory. "Deal."

Finley let out a breath, relieved. Getting outside would give them time to observe more of the human world and the opportunity to bring Julie back to the hollow. The sooner they completed their task, the sooner they could return to the safety of the grove.

Ethan's father reached for the plate of bacon, serving himself another helping before offering it to Ethan. Finley hesitated for a moment before shaking their head, refusing the strips of fried fat. The greasy smell was overwhelming. The thought of putting it in their mouth made their stomach turn. But Ethan loved bacon.

"More for me then," Mr. Danvers replied with a shrug.

Julie raised an eyebrow. "Since when do you not eat bacon?"

Finley scrambled for an excuse. "Just not hungry for it today."

Julie snorted. "Yeah, right."

To compensate, Finley went back for the syrup, watching the sweet liquid pool across the pancake and run off the side, the fluffy bread having long been saturated. The thick, amber substance reminded them of the root nectar they drank at home. They took a bite, then another as the mélange of flavors grew on them until they found themselves holding the plate up to their face, licking every last drop from the surface. The sweetness was intoxicating, almost dizzying.

Finley looked up from their plate to find the entire family staring at them.

"Okay. That was disgusting," said Julie.

Finley wiped their mouth with the back of their hand, forgoing the napkin under their elbow, and forced out a nervous laugh. "Guess I was hungrier than I thought."

The air outside was thick with humidity, the sun hanging low in the late morning sky as Julie led the way down the cracked sidewalk. She rode with confidence, gripping the handlebars of her bike and glancing over her shoulder at Ethan, who lagged a few yards behind. She couldn't remember the last time Ethan didn't fight her for the lead when they were out together.

"You're acting weird," she said. "Like, weirder than usual."

Finley had anticipated that. They forced a laugh, trying to replicate the casual ease Ethan would have with his sister. "What do you mean? I'm just tired," they said. "Didn't sleep great last night."

"Uh-huh," she replied, unconvinced, as she slowed to his speed. "Well, don't fall asleep in the lake and drown. That'd be a real buzzkill."

The tires hummed against the pavement as the siblings coasted side by side, the warm summer air blowing against their faces. Julie pointed down the road ahead, where a few other kids from school rode in the same direction.

"Looks like everyone's going to the lake today," she said. "We should hurry before all the good spots are taken."

Finley pedaled lazily, watching as the group disappeared around the bend. "The lake's always the same, though. Muddy water and too many kids splashing around." He glanced up toward the hill, where the roofline of the orphanage was visible above the trees. "What if we went somewhere different instead?"

Julie gave him a side-eye. "Different like where?"

They pedaled in silence for a moment until the orphanage came back into view during a break in the tree line. The second-floor windows of the abandoned building loomed large, like a pair of eyes watching the town below. When they spoke again, Finley was careful with their words.

"Don't you ever wonder what's in there?" they said, motioning to the old building. "Everyone talks about it, but no one's actually been inside."

Julie snorted, kicking her pedals to surge ahead. "No. And you shouldn't, either. It's condemned for a reason."

Finley matched her pace. "But think about it. What are the chances of the ball landing in that tiny window? Don't you want to check it out?"

Julie slammed on her brakes, skidding to a stop. Her eyes narrowed at him. "What's gotten into you? First at dinner the other night, now this. You've been acting like a freak about that place ever since the game. Don't worry about what those jerks said. You don't have to prove anything to them. It's just a stupid baseball," she said firmly. "You don't risk tetanus and falling debris for that. That ball was worthless anyway."

"It's not that," Finley replied. "What if it's not just an open window? Everyone says it's haunted...."

"What? You heard those ghost stories again and now you're obsessed? It's not haunted, Ethan."

"You don't know that," Finley said quickly. "There's gotta be some truth to those old stories. Maybe those kids who went missing are still there. What if we find something? Something important."

Julie groaned. "Forget it. We're not going to that creepy, abandoned orphanage, okay? We're going to the lake, we're going to hang out with actual living people, and you are going to stop acting like a total weirdo. No wonder the other kids pick on you." She pushed off again, leaving him behind in a spray of gravel.

Finley clenched their jaw, frustration simmering beneath their skin. Humans were so stubborn, so unwilling to listen to things beyond their understanding. They needed Julie to accompany them to the orphanage, but pushing too hard would only make her more suspicious.

They forced a grin. "Whatever. It was just a suggestion. We can go to the lake."

With her back to her brother, Julie rolled her eyes, continuing to pedal as she muttered something under her breath. Finley followed, swallowing their irritation. The orphanage would have to wait. But not for long.

CHAPTER 13

Finley and Julie heard echoes of laughter coming from the lake as they rode their bikes down the trail. The lively conversation pushed Julie and, in turn, Finley to pedal harder so as not to miss out on any more of the fun. They emerged from the woods and pulled into the clearing to find a group of kids already gathered on the shore, their voices carrying through the warm summer air.

Maggie, Noah, and Connor were among them, standing near a cooler filled with sodas and snacks. Another group chased each other in the water, causing ripples in the lake's naturally smooth surface. The air carried an aroma of damp earth and sunscreen.

Finley hesitated for a moment before following Julie, carefully adjusting their expression to mimic Ethan's demeanor. Every movement felt deliberate, their posture awkward as they attempted to blend in.

"Hey, you guys made it," Maggie called, waving them over.

As the newcomers descended the slope toward the others, Noah and Connor whispered something to each other. Then Noah picked up a frisbee and launched it at Ethan. "Think fast!" he yelled, hoping to catch the boy off-guard.

But Finley's instinct kicked in and they leaped off the ground, catching the frisbee on one finger and landing in a dramatic fashion, the disc spinning on their outstretched digit.

Everyone stopped what they were doing, including the kids playing in the water, to stare at Ethan's surprising display of athletic prowess.

"Nice catch, man," blurted out Connor, who received a glare from his companion for the remark. Ignoring Noah's scowl, Connor continued. "Between that and your big hit at the game the other day, you might not be so bad after all."

"Thanks, I guess," Finley replied.

Maggie nudged Noah. "You gonna invite him to your party or what?"

Noah shifted uncomfortably. "Uh, yeah. I guess you can come if you want," he said, barely meeting Finley's eyes.

Maggie shot him a look. "Don't make it sound so enthusiastic. Geez."

Connor cut in to break the tension. "He's still pissed about the home run the other day. He'll get over it. It was a great hit."

Finley nodded, forcing a smile. "Thanks. Sounds fun."

Julie grabbed a soda from the cooler and cracked it open. "So, what's the plan? We just roasting under the sun or actually doing something?"

Noah grinned. "We were about to start a game. You in?"

"Depends. What game?" Julie asked.

"Shark," Maggie said. "One person's the shark, and they have to catch the others in the water. If you get tagged, you become a shark too. Last one left wins."

"Classic," Julie said approvingly. "I'm in."

Maggie turned to Ethan. "What about you?"

Finley's stomach twisted. The lake stretched out before them was dark and murky, unlike the crystal clear water in Finley's hollow. Something about it made their skin crawl, though they couldn't quite place why. Their intuition told them to avoid it. Finley shook their head. "I think I'll just watch."

Connor shot him a look. "What, afraid of lake monsters?"

"Maybe he just can't swim," Noah said, smirking.

Julie rolled her eyes. "Of course he can swim. Ethan, stop being a baby and get in."

Finley hesitated. More eyes were on them, waiting, expecting. If they refused, it would be strange—suspicious even. It was something Ethan would do. He would dive in without a second thought. Finley couldn't afford to draw any more attention their way.

They took a breath and waded in.

The moment their skin met the water, a searing pain shot up their legs. It was as if the lake itself had turned to acid. Finley clenched their teeth, trying to keep their expression neutral as they took another step into the lake. Their calves continued to burn, the pain intensifying every moment they remained submerged until they couldn't bear the agony any longer.

Stumbling backward out of the water, they nearly lost their balance in the process. Their breath came in short gasps as they forced themselves onto the shore, the pain still radiating beneath their skin. Their legs were stained red, their flesh raw, where the water had touched them.

"Dude, are you okay?" Maggie asked, stepping closer.

Julie's eyes widened as she rushed over to him. "Ethan, what the hell? You look like you stepped into boiling water."

"Maybe he's allergic to something in the lake," Connor suggested. "That happens, right?"

Finley could barely hear them. Their mind reeled from the agonizing pain. They couldn't think about anything else. It was a pain they had felt before. Only one thing would cause such a reaction. They hadn't considered that the water might be tainted with iron.

For a moment, Finley felt themself shift, as if they were about to revert back to their true form right there in front of everyone. If that happened, everything would be ruined. Luckily, the feeling passed, although the burning sensation persisted. They needed to leave.

"I—I don't feel great," they mumbled, backing away. "I think I need to go home."

Without waiting for a response, they turned and sprinted up the path leading back to the house, forgetting their bike and ignoring Julie's calls to wait up. They had played the part as long as they could for the time being, but this world was filled with dangers Finley hadn't considered. They should have trusted their instincts. Now the entire group would be talking about them.

While the fraught scene unfolded, Ethan's reaction to the lake water held the attention of everyone on the shore. With the children focused on Ethan, the rustling in the bushes went unnoticed as Eliza backed away from the clearing. Since finding the broken fence at the orphanage, she had kept a close eye on the children, waiting for the imposter to reveal itself. After what she just witnessed, the culprit's identity was no longer in question.

But how to proceed? Kill the changeling before it stole another child? The town would crucify her for the transgression. With Gene Bell's crusade against her, she stood first in line to be accused. Although she would gladly trade her freedom to stop the creature, she couldn't allow herself to be taken from her post. Not now. If she was no longer free to keep watch over the town, who would remain to prevent more of its kind from emerging and stalking the children of Fairfield?

She scurried through the woods, back to her house, ignoring the branches clawing at her sleeves and the clumps of mud sticking to her shoes. Her mind was already buzzing, sorting through the preparations required before her inevitable confrontation with the changeling. She had little time to waste, for the creature would not rest and she had much to do.

The house was empty when Finley returned. They were thankful Ethan's parents had already left for work. If either of them saw Finley come home early or, even worse, the burns on their legs, questions would swirl. The marks would send Ethan's mother into a panic if she spotted them. Their secret was unraveling too soon. The timeline would have to be quickened before they were discovered.

With the coast clear, Finley stripped off their clothes and inspected their damaged legs. The skin was already blistering. They wasted no time jumping into the cold shower, using a washcloth to gently clean their legs, wiping away any of the poisonous residue that remained. The injury would heal, but Finley could do nothing about their damaged reputation except wait and hope the other children forgot what they saw.

They had never encountered anything as repulsive as iron. They knew enough to stay away from the hardened metal but hadn't considered the foul substance would be present in the lake. It was more than just a dislike or even an allergy. Iron repelled them like a magnetic field. The aversion was woven into the very fabric of their being. The scent alone, metallic and sharp, made their skin prickle with unease. The touch of it was unbearable, like pressing their hand against burning embers. Even being near it made their head feel heavy and their limbs sluggish, as if the planet's gravity suddenly tripled.

Instinctually, they avoided it, their movements always subtly steering them away from rusted fences, cast-iron pans, and even the silverware at the dinner table. Finley knew, deep in their borrowed bones, that iron was dangerous. The iron fence had kept them sealed in their prison for years until the roots were able to penetrate the barrier. Next time they ventured out, they would need to be more careful, even if it meant deviating from Ethan's expected behavior.

CHAPTER 14

The next morning, before leaving for work, Ethan's mother knocked gently on his bedroom door. After receiving no reply, she slowly pushed it open. The room sat still and dark. The rising sun's faint glow penetrating the closed shades provided the only illumination. She expected to find Ethan asleep, but he sat cross-legged on the bed. His back was straight, his hands resting unnaturally on his knees. His eyes were open, but he made no acknowledgement of her presence. She followed his line of sight to the wall covered in posters, but his gaze seemed to look through them. If she didn't know better, she might have thought he was lost in a state of deep meditation.

She spoke his name, snapping him out of his trance. He turned his head toward her, but his expression remained unreadable.

Julie had told her about what happened at the lake, that something happened to Ethan when he went in the water, how he rushed out immediately, his skin red and irritated, and ran home without a word. Julie said it looked like some kind of allergic reaction. That made sense, she supposed, but a reaction to what? He had swum in that lake for years, and nothing like that had ever happened to him before. And if there was something in the water, how come it didn't affect any of the other children?

She was glad he didn't seem to be seriously hurt, but as she stood in the doorway, studying her son, an uneasy feeling weighed heavily on her.

"You feeling okay?" she asked as she stepped into his room.

"I'm fine," Finley replied, but the words lacked warmth and did little to allay Mrs. Danvers's concern.

She frowned. "Julie said you left your bike and ran all the way home. That's not fine, Ethan. She had to ask for help bringing it back for you."

They hesitated before answering as if trying to decide what the right response should be. "Sorry. It was the water," they said finally. "It didn't feel right. But I'm okay now."

Ethan's mother sighed, walking farther into the room but stopping when a peculiar odor hit her senses—the scent of something earthy and damp, like overturned soil after a heavy rain. It didn't smell bad, exactly, but it was strange for a bedroom. She wrinkled her nose.

"Have you been tracking mud in here?" she asked, glancing around. "When was the last time you cleaned?"

Finley held their breath, hoping Ethan's mother didn't come any closer. "I don't know."

She shook her head. "Well, can you please tidy up today so I can vacuum in here?" She waited for a groan, an eye-roll, some kind of protest.

Instead, Finley nodded once. "Okay," they replied.

That was too easy. She usually had to resort to bribes to get him to do any chores. Something was off. Maybe the water affected him more than he was letting on. "Let me take a look at your legs."

"I told you I'm fine, Mom," Finley replied in a snippy tone, pulling their legs close to their body.

Mrs. Danvers decided not to press the issue, for now. She shifted her stance, bringing her hands out from behind her back. She held out a stack of video games that had been hidden behind her the entire time. "By the way, since you came home on time yesterday, and with everything that happened at the lake, I figured you could have these back. Thought you'd be happy to rest today and play your games." She held them out, waiting for him to light up like he always did.

But he didn't.

His gaze flickered over them briefly before turning his attention back toward the wall. No excitement, no smile. Just another blank expression.

"You don't want them?" she asked, forcing a small laugh. "Since when?"

He hesitated. "Not right now."

Her stomach twisted. "Then what are you planning to do today? Besides cleaning your room, of course."

"I want to go out with Julie."

The reply was immediate, so quick it almost felt like a preprogrammed response. It was the first thing she heard him say with any real interest in days. It seemed strange that he suddenly wanted to hang out with his sister.

"Julie's busy today. She already went with Maggie over to Noah's house. I guess he's having a party tonight? They went to help him set up."

For a split second, she swore she saw something flicker across his face—a flash of disappointment or frustration. But then it was gone and his expression returned to the neutral state she had found him in.

"Oh," he said, accepting the situation.

That was when Mrs. Danvers realized it wasn't about going out with Julie. He wanted an excuse to see Maggie. She found it sweet that he had a crush on his childhood friend but hoped he didn't do anything to ruin the friendship.

She stared at him for a moment, and an unexpected shiver ran down her back. She forced herself to shake off the uneasy feeling and placed the games on his desk. "Well, I've gotta get going to work. Try to get some rest and don't forget to clean this cave up a bit," she said, resisting the urge to open his shades.

"Okay," he said plainly.

She gave him one last lingering glance before stepping out into the hallway. But even as she closed the door behind her, the troubled feeling didn't leave. She knew something was wrong with Ethan. There was something different about him, and it was more than just teenage apathy.

Sheriff Cahill had just sat down for lunch when he heard the low whirring of a struggling engine approaching his house. He didn't need to look out the window to know whose vehicle the rumble belonged to. Gene Bell's rusted old truck sputtered and coughed as it rolled up the gravel driveway.

Bruce sighed, setting down his half-eaten turkey sandwich and wiping his hands on a napkin. He had tried his best to be a friend to Gene over the years and was always willing to lend him an ear, but Gene didn't come by for social calls and Bruce preferred the man save his conspiracy theories for when he was on the clock rather than interrupting his time at home. With Noah's friends over helping him set up for the party later that evening, the last thing he needed was for Gene to make a scene in front of them. After the direction of their last conversation, Bruce had grown concerned for his friend, but he knew any attempt to placate the man's festering rage would be taken as indifference toward his missing daughters. Every time it looked like Gene was ready to move on with his life, he fell back into his pit of anger and despair.

Through the kitchen window, he saw the truck jerk to a stop and the driver's side door swing open before Gene even killed the engine. Climbing out of the truck, Gene moved with the urgency of a man on a mission.

Bruce pushed himself up from the table and made his way to the front door as Gene stomped up the porch steps. "Jesus, Gene," Bruce muttered, squinting against the glare of the late-morning sun as he scanned the visitor from head to toe. "You look like hell."

Gene ignored the comment, his eyes fierce as they shifted from side to side. "She's at it again," he said.

The sheriff scowled as the smell of alcohol on Gene's breath wafted in his face. "You been drinkin' already, Gene?"

"Damnit, Bruce. This is serious," he grumbled.

The sheriff sighed. "Who's at it again?" He knew who Gene was talking about, of course, but figured he would play along. There was only one person in town on the receiving end of Gene's relentless accusations.

"Eliza Wilkins, who else?" he replied impatiently. "I caught her poking around the orphanage again last night. She was performing some sorta ritual."

Bruce scrunched his forehead. "What do you mean?"

"Hell if I know, but I confronted her to put an end to her witchcraft, and that's when she threatened the kids, talking about kidnapping 'em. Figured I should tell you before it's too late."

Although he knew better than to buy into Gene's wild stories, he couldn't ignore a threat, no matter how trivial it seemed—not after what had happened last time. "Which kids? What exactly did she say? Think carefully, Gene. Her exact words are important."

"She said they were all in danger. That more would wind up missing soon. I'm telling you, she's up to something. Someone's gotta put a stop to her before she takes any more kids."

"Whoa, hold up a second. You can't say things like that. You know we never found anything connecting her to Sarah and Liz's disappearance."

Just hearing their names made Gene's eyes bulge in anger. "You just don't get it. She can't be allowed to roam our town any longer. Someone's gotta put a stop to her, and if you won't—"

"Cool it," the sheriff said forcefully, cutting him off. "We've talked about this before. You know you can't take the law into your own hands. I try to do well by you, but the limits of our friendship only extend so far."

From the living room, the conversation between the kids came to a hush. Noah, Maggie, Connor, and Julie had been sitting around doing more chatting than any actual preparations for the party. With Gene's raised voice and irate temper, they couldn't help but overhear the exchange.

"Witch?" Maggie mouthed to Connor, remembering their strange interaction with the woman a few days prior.

They had all heard rumors about Eliza Wilkins, but none of them thought she was actually dangerous. However, the mention of witchcraft and a ritual certainly caught their attention.

Gene's voice rose again from the other room. "There's something unnatural going on, and she's at the center of it."

The sheriff held up his hands. "Gene..."

"Damnit, Bruce, she's up to no good," Gene continued, "just like last time, and you're not gonna do anything about it."

"That's enough," Bruce said, stepping onto the porch and pulling the door shut behind him so the kids wouldn't hear any more of the man's ravings.

Inside, the children ran to the window and leaned onto it, straining to listen to the adults' conversation.

"Gene, I'm only gonna say this once," Bruce said, keeping his voice level. "You need to back off. You said she made a threat, so I'll head down to her place and talk to her, but it's gonna have to wait. I'm off duty today. My son is having some friends over tonight. So if you don't mind, I need to help him prepare for his get-together."

Gene hesitated, glancing past the sheriff where he could see shadows of the kids trying to eavesdrop in the window. Lowering his voice, he said, "You can ignore me all you want, Bruce, but we both know something's coming. You're just scared to admit it."

Bruce folded his arms. "The only thing I'm scared of is you running your mouth and getting people riled up over nothing. Now, I've let you say your piece, but you need to get in your truck and go. I said I'll talk to her."

With a final glare, Gene turned and stomped back to his vehicle. The old engine groaned as he started it up, the exhaust spitting a puff of black smoke before the truck pulled out of the driveway.

Inside, the kids exchanged uneasy glances.

"You hear that?" Maggie whispered.

"Do you think we're actually in danger?" Julie asked.

"Naw," Noah replied confidently. "That nut job has been coming around accusing her of shit forever. I wouldn't pay any attention to him."

"But we heard Eliza saying the same thing in the woods the other day, remember?" Maggie said.

The children pondered the old man's words for a moment before Noah broke the silence. "Seems like almost everyone in this town has a few screws loose," he replied smugly. "I wouldn't trust either of those two as far as I could spit."

CHAPTER 15

The party was already in full swing when Finley and Julie arrived at Connor's house later that evening. Electronic music pulsed from the backyard, where they heard murmurs of laughter along with water splashing in the pool. The smell of grilled meat accompanied the sounds, causing Julie's stomach to rumble in hunger and Finley's to turn in disgust. The imposter prayed they wouldn't be forced to eat any more animal flesh in an attempt to fit in. They had barely been able to choke down a few bites at home without raising suspicion.

The two lingered for a moment at the edge of the yard, wondering if they should ring the doorbell or go around through the side gate. Having been there earlier to set up, Julie led the way through the gate.

As they entered the backyard full of people, everyone turned to glance at the new arrivals before returning to their conversations. Groups of kids were scattered across the lawn, some laughing loudly, others huddled in smaller circles, swapping gossip and inside jokes. A few others swam in the immaculately maintained in-ground pool in the center of the yard.

Finley immediately thought of the incident at the lake. The water looked much cleaner than the dirty lake they foolishly waded into the previous day, but they would take no chances. They looked around the yard, their posture rigid as they took in the gathering and fought off feelings of estrangement.

Julie, on the other hand, had no trouble joining in. She waved at a group of kids sitting at a picnic table and turned to Finley with a grin. "Just try not to be too weird, okay?" she teased, nudging them with her elbow.

Finley gave her a blank look.

"You know, less standing around like a statue with that dumb look on your face," she added. "Try to act like you're actually having a good time for a change."

Before they could respond, Maggie appeared from the crowd, her eyes lighting up when she saw them. "You made it!"

Julie gave her a hug while Finley attempted, unsuccessfully, to take their sister's advice.

"Julie wouldn't let me stay home," Finley said, earning an exasperated look from the girls.

"Good. Where's the fun in that?" Maggie replied. "I'm glad you came. We need more people who know how to have fun."

From behind her, Noah scoffed. "Not sure he qualifies."

Finley turned toward him. "What's that supposed to mean?"

Noah leaned back against the picnic table, crossing his arms. "Just saying you don't exactly scream life of the party. Sometimes I wonder if you forgot how to talk."

Julie opened her mouth to snap back, but Finley held up a hand, stopping her. Instead of a reply, they reached into their pocket and pulled out a baseball.

Noah's eyes lit up when he saw it.

Connor leaped up from his seat at the table for a better look. "No way! Is that—?"

"From the orphanage," Finley confirmed, tossing it lightly toward Noah.

"You actually went in there?" Maggie asked, a mixture of surprise and intrigue in her voice.

"What does it look like?" Finley said.

Connor whistled slowly. "That's pretty badass. I didn't think you had it in you."

For the first time, Finley felt the tension between them and their peers shift. Even Noah seemed to reassess them.

"Alright," Noah said, nodding in approval as he inspected the ball in his hands. "Maybe you're not as boring as I thought."

Finley smirked slightly. "I'll take that as a compliment."

"So what's it like in there?" Maggie asked curiously. "As scary as it's made out to be?"

"It's kinda cool, actually," they replied. "Like you're stepping into another world."

By that point, a large group had gathered around to hear the tale of Finley's expedition. The air between them lightened, and just like that, they were one step closer to blending in.

To Maggie's surprise, the party continued without a hitch. Her friends, who normally mixed like chocolate and cheese, were suddenly acting like besties. They gorged themselves on pizza, danced to the DJ's rotating beats, and played an assortment of games for the next several hours until the party began to wind down.

With their curfew approaching and their houses only a short walk away, Maggie, Julie, and Finley took off down the street together, wishing the remaining partygoers goodnight before they departed.

Julie walked ahead, sensing a spark between her brother and Maggie. She hummed to herself as she scrolled through her phone, allowing them some privacy. She knew Ethan had long pined over their neighbor, but this was the first time Maggie had shown any return interest.

The pair lagged behind, the cool night air swirling between them.

"You really went into the orphanage, huh?" Maggie said after a moment.

Finley nodded. "Yeah."

"Alone?"

"Yeah."

She studied her friend, trying to read his expression. The Ethan she knew would have never gone into that orphanage by himself, at least the Ethan she thought she knew. But she wasn't complaining. Something about the new Ethan intrigued her. For the first time, she pictured him as possibly more than just a childhood friend.

"You weren't scared?" she asked.

Finley considered that. They weren't sure if fear was something they felt the way humans did. They were cautious, yes, but scared? Still, they had to consider how Ethan felt in that moment. Finley pictured the expression on the boy's face as they emerged from the shadows and the look in his eyes as his body withered away.

"Maybe a little," they admitted.

Maggie smirked. "Figures."

"Would you want to check it out?" they asked.

Maggie hesitated, the stories she heard all her life flashing through her head. "Right now? It's gotta be pitch black in there."

Up ahead, Julie's ears perked up. She was trying not to eavesdrop on their conversation but couldn't help overhearing her brother's suggestion. The mention of the detour triggered her memory of his attempt to bring her to the abandoned building the day before. If he had already been there to find the ball, that could explain his lack of fear. But what had he seen that made him so eager to return?

Julie stopped in the middle of the street between their houses and turned back to look at her companions. Both of them wore big smiles on their faces. She couldn't remember the last time she saw Ethan that happy. The pair walked next to each other, their hands almost touching as they swung back and forth with each step. She gave them a wave and returned her attention to her screen while she headed up the walkway. "See you guys tomorrow," she said before disappearing inside, hoping not to interrupt their moment or make things awkward.

Finley and Maggie lingered in the road. The street was empty, the row of houses dark. A single streetlamp buzzed above them, casting a golden glow around their shadows on the pavement.

"I thought I had you figured out, but you're more complex than you seem," Maggie said, tilting her head as she looked at her neighbor.

Finley pursed their lips. "And what did you expect?"

She shrugged. "I don't know. Someone quieter, more... I don't know, closed off, I guess."

"Maybe I still am."

She took a step closer, her presence warm despite the night's chill. "You're kind of a mystery, you know that?"

"And you like mysteries?"

She smirked. "Maybe."

Finley inhaled deeply, tasting the human's overwhelming scent. The smell made their stomach twist in a knot. They were still disgusted by it, but beneath the off-putting odor was something else, something that made them lean in for another whiff before they could think better of it.

Maggie noticed Finley's movement and replied in kind until they met. The kiss was soft and uncertain.

Finley inhaled sharply but didn't pull away. Instead, they pressed closer, their hands brushing her arm. For a brief moment, Finley almost recoiled, but the strange sensation pulled them nearer still as the wet warmth of her tongue fit against theirs until a deep hunger stirred inside, reminding them of their purpose.

They withdrew first, masking their growing appetite.

Maggie blinked up at them, breathless. "That was..."

"Yeah."

She smiled, amused by their lack of words. "I should get home."

Finley hesitated. "Or..."

Maggie raised an eyebrow.

Finley glanced down the road, toward the place that had been calling to them since the moment they arrived in the town. The orphanage sat at the edge of the woods, waiting in the shadows for their return.

Maggie followed their gaze, then looked back at them, a spark of mischief in her eyes. "You really want to go back there, don't you?"

Finley didn't answer, but they didn't have to.

Maggie let out a breathy laugh. "Alright, let's go. My phone has a flashlight. But we have to be quick. I was supposed to be home ten minutes ago."

They turned together, walking in the night toward the one place she had been warned away from her entire life.

Fairfield Gazzette ^{50¢}

Early Edition   Fairfield's First Choice for News Since 1926   Vol. 32 No. 10

January 7, 1982

FORMER ORPHANAGE HEADMASTER FOUND DEAD IN OFFICE

The troubled former headmaster of Fairfield Children's Home, Patrick Brennan, was found deceased late Sunday inside his locked office at the now-vacant facility. Authorities ruled the death an apparent suicide.

A note recovered near the body blamed the missing children on "little green men" and apologized for his involvement in the child trafficking scheme.

Sheriff Cahill declined further comment, adding that the town "would do well to let the past rest."

The property will remain closed indefinitely.

CHAPTER 16

The phone rang early in the Danvers' household, breaking the quiet that hung over the halls. Ethan's mother, still only half awake and scrolling through her social media feed, looked at the caller ID.

Mr. Danvers groaned as he rolled over to check the time. "Who the hell is calling you this early?" he grumbled.

Ignoring her husband, she cleared her throat before answering the phone. "Hello?"

"April, it's Jane, from across the street." The woman's voice cracked as she spoke, a frantic tone in her words. "Is Maggie there?"

She took a moment to respond, her head still foggy from the early hour and lack of coffee. "I... I don't think so. The kids are still sleeping. What's going on?"

The reply came with a whimper. "She never came home last night."

April frowned. The news sent a jolt of energy through her, and she sat up in bed, suddenly no longer groggy.

"What? I thought she went to the party at Noah's house with the other kids."

"She did. But that was the last we'd heard from her. She would have messaged me if there had been a problem. She isn't answering her phone. I called around this morning. Noah said she left the party with Julie and Ethan. I thought maybe..." Jane's voice wavered. "Please tell me she's there."

"Let me go check with the kids. Hold on a minute."

Mrs. Danvers slipped out of bed. Her husband, fully awake after having overheard pieces of the conversation, listened intently for more details. April gave him a worried look as she left the room to check on the children.

She padded quickly down the hall and went to Julie's room first. Her daughter was still fast asleep after the eventful evening the night before. Covering the receiver of her phone, she nudged her daughter gently. "Julie, wake up, honey."

Julie stirred, rubbing her eyes. "Mom? What's wrong?"

"Did Maggie stay over last night?"

Julie blinked, shaking her head as the fog of sleep cleared. "No. I don't think so," she replied, thinking about their walk home from the party. "Have you asked—" She stopped mid-sentence as Ethan crept silently into the doorway.

Mrs. Danvers saw Julie's eyes shift focus and turned to face her son. Finley stepped fully into view, a knot rising in their throat as they prepared for the interrogation.

"Ethan, did you hear that? Is Maggie here? She never made it home from the party last night."

Finley remained stoic, keeping their gaze locked on Julie, only shaking their head no in reply.

"Do you know where she could be?" Mrs. Danvers pressed. "Her mother is worried sick."

Again, Finley shook their head, offering no further response.

Julie returned Finley's stare, waiting for them to give some sort of explanation. When it became apparent they wouldn't, she interjected. "We all walked home together. She was right outside. I went in, but Maggie—"

Finley's gaze hardened, a fierce look in their eyes, but they remained composed. They cut off Julie before she could continue. "We all went in together. She was walking up the steps to her house when we left her."

Julie almost contradicted her brother, but something stopped her from speaking up. He was hiding something. But why would he lie?

Mrs. Danvers noticed the strained look between the siblings and scrunched her nose, studying her son. "Are you sure?"

Finley nodded, their expression calm and practiced. "She went home."

Mrs. Danvers's attention returned to the phone in her hand. Her heart sank further, dreading having to tell Mrs. Evans the bad news.

Placing the receiver back to her ear, April's voice was strained. "Jane, she's not here. Neither of the kids have seen her since last night. They all walked home together, so I don't know what could have happened."

Jane audibly whimpered at the news, memories of the town's history of missing children flashing through her head. The fact that none of those children were ever found clawed at her already fragile mental state. "Phil's out looking for her now," she said. "I don't know what to do. I've called everyone." Jane's voice was barely a whisper. "No one has seen her."

"Try not to panic," Mrs. Danvers replied, attempting to infuse her voice with a sense of confidence she didn't possess. "There's gotta be an explanation. I'm sure she'll turn up. We'll get dressed and be right over to help look."

"Thank you," Maggie's mom said before the line went dead.

A soft knock sounded at the door. April turned to see her husband standing there, concern etched on his face. "What's going on?"

April spoke quietly, a grave look on her face. "Maggie's missing. She never made it home last night."

By mid-morning, a search party had assembled at the Evans' house. Sheriff Cahill coordinated the volunteers. His demeanor remained calm but authoritative as he disseminated instructions to the group. Although he put on his best game face for the crowd, his eyes betrayed his growing unease. He was hopeful they would find Maggie safe, but he couldn't help thinking history was repeating itself, again.

The town had been through this before. Memories of long days spent searching with nothing to show for it came rushing back. Each day ended the same, with no answers or happy endings. He was still dealing with the consequences so many years later. His mind returned to Gene's visit and the allegations against Eliza. He should have dropped what he was doing and went to question her immediately, but Gene was hardly a reliable source of information and it was his day off.

The next morning, just as Gene had predicted, a child was missing. One of his son's friends, no less. Maybe it was just a coincidence, but Bruce had a sick feeling in his stomach that things were only going to get worse before they got better. By looking at the faces in the crowd before him, he knew they harbored the same fear.

Julie and Ethan stood on their porch across the street as they watched the people gathering in Maggie's yard. They had offered to assist in the search, but for safety reasons, all children had been ordered to stay indoors. Without knowing what they were up against, fears of a child predator or worse kept everyone paranoid and overprotective.

The siblings were about to go back inside when Sheriff Cahill wrapped up his instructions to the search party and called them over to the group.

"You kids were the last to see Maggie," he said as they approached. "Is there anything you remember that might help us find her? Anywhere she might have gone after you parted ways?"

Ethan shook his head. "No, sir. We all made it home from the party together. She was headed up her walkway as I went in."

The sheriff's brow furrowed in thought as he inspected the boy's manner and considered his words.

Julie hesitated, glancing at her brother. She looked like she wanted to speak but remained silent. She knew Ethan wasn't being completely honest with the sheriff, but she didn't know why. Without knowing his motive, she didn't want to contradict him in front of everyone. There was no point stirring up panic and her brother's ire for what could very well be nothing. She needed to talk to Ethan alone, to understand what truly happened after she left them.

Realizing he wasn't getting anything useful from the kids, Sheriff Cahill told them to go inside but to notify him immediately if they thought of anything that might be helpful. They were about to return to their house when a murmur in the crowd caught the group's attention. The sheriff turned to the cause of the commotion and saw a new arrival making her way through the group.

News traveled fast through the small town, and with a child missing, old rumors and speculation returned. Eliza Wilkins took the opportunity to make herself known to the gathering, mumbling a warning to the townsfolk. Bruce was planning to stop by her house as soon as the search party dispersed. Although he still wasn't convinced she was involved in the disappearance, he couldn't ignore the coincidence of Gene's allegation paired with a missing child. He owed it to Maggie's parents and the rest of the town to discover the truth. Although her arrival made that task easier for him, he would've preferred to have had the discussion without so many prying eyes.

The sheriff approached her before the woman's appearance caused any more disturbance. "Eliza, just the woman I was hoping to see."

"Gathering your pitchforks to blame an innocent old woman for another disappearance again, are we?" she murmured, shifting her gaze from side to side, each of the volunteers looking away as she eyed them intently.

"Children wandering off, never to be seen again. This town has seen it before. Surely you, of all people, know the consequences of inaction."

Sheriff Cahill sighed, rubbing his forehead. "I don't have time for your riddles, Eliza. If you know anything about what happened to Maggie, now's your chance to speak up."

She ignored him, scanning the faces in the crowd, lingering on Ethan, the only one besides the sheriff who met her gaze. "Secrets have a way of surfacing, and imposters can only hide in plain sight for so long."

Finley's face paled but remained composed. It felt as if the woman spoke directly to them. They shrank away, hoping no one else noticed the old woman's focus, but Julie's suspicions had already sprouted and she studied the interaction carefully.

Eliza continued her sermon. "If it is the girl you seek, then waste not your steps in the woods or the streets of this town. This is not my first warning, but deaf ears make for heavy grief. The hour for salvation has passed. The seal has been undone. The girl has been taken from this realm, and it may be too late to save her. The answers you seek rest within the old orphanage. But know this—though the walls remain, the girl within them does not."

The crowd stood quietly except for a few nervous murmurs as they attempted to make sense of the old woman's words. Sheriff Cahill broke the silence, clearing his throat loudly before calling for attention. "Alright, let's try to stay focused on the task. Eliza, if you have any concrete information, please see me privately. As for everyone else, if you haven't been assigned to a group, see Deputy Rick and we'll fit you in right away. Time is of the essence."

Bruce didn't know if he could trust a word out of Eliza's mouth, but he couldn't just ignore her warning, not again. Even if she wasn't involved in the disappearance, maybe she knew something. But he didn't appreciate her games. The last thing he needed was her wild conspiracy theories sending the townsfolk into a panic. Either way, the orphanage had to be searched, and the sheriff knew that job fell to him.

As the crowd dispersed, Julie pulled Ethan aside, her voice a harsh whisper. "We need to talk."

Finley nodded, their expression unreadable. "Lead the way."

Sheriff Cahill stood at the threshold of the old orphanage with his most trusted deputy by his side. The search party had spread out across town, combing every familiar spot Maggie could have gone. The largest group of volunteers remained near the girl's house to scour the surrounding woods, but between the rumors circulating the old building and Eliza's insistence that the house was tied to the disappearance, Bruce knew a thorough search of the orphanage was required.

At the time of Gene's daughters' disappearance, Eliza claimed ignorance. It wasn't until much later that she shifted the blame to strange creatures from the woods. By then, the sheriff had already stopped listening. Yet there he was, following up on leads he should have looked into decades ago.

For safety reasons, he preferred not to have the volunteers traipsing around the dilapidated building. Not to mention, if Eliza's fears turned out to be true, he needed to keep the crime scene undisturbed. So while the volunteers scoured the town, he headed up to the abandoned building, hoping to put the rumors to rest.

As expected, they found the perimeter gate secure, but their relief was short-lived. Just beyond the entrance, a mangled section of fencing sagged outward, its metal twisted and torn as if something had forced its way through. The officers stopped to inspect it, exchanging uneasy looks while the sheriff radioed in the damage. After a moment, they continued toward the main building. Bruce pulled out the key for the front entrance, then slowed when he saw the door already cracked open. He paused, thinking back to his last visit. He knew with certainty that it had been locked on his previous trip to the building.

The open door and broken fence made him think of Eliza's claims and he suddenly wondered if she wasn't as crazy as everyone made her out to be. Although he doubted the place was filled with alien creatures, as she implied, the prospect of a squatter or wild animal remained at the forefront of his mind.

With the possibility of a kidnapper or killer inside, the sheriff drew his service weapon and nodded at his deputy. Using the tip of his boot, he nudged the door open, wincing as the rusted metal hinges screeched. The orphanage had always been an eyesore, but looking inside the dim hall, he realized the building was in worse shape than he remembered. Vines crept along the interior like veins, emerging through the cracked walls and boarded-up windows. The entire structure was in an advanced state of decay. The air was thick with the smell of rotting wood and decomposing vegetation that permeated the building.

He stepped inside cautiously, the floor groaning under his weight. The light from the doorway barely penetrated the darkness, revealing only glimpses of sagging ceilings and piles of debris. The sheriff pulled out his flashlight and swept the beam across the ruined interior. What once had been a grand entryway was reduced to a deteriorating husk of rotting floorboards and water-stained walls. The orphanage had been abandoned for decades, but it looked as though nature reclaimed it with unsettling speed.

"Hello?" he called, his voice echoing through the hollow corridors. "Maggie?"

He glanced at his deputy and shrugged, moving deeper into the building, his partner close behind. He stopped at every room, shining his light into each corner as he went. Every time he saw a flash of movement in an illuminated room, a closer inspection revealed nothing but shadows dancing in the light.

Many of the rooms still held remnants of the past. Everywhere he looked, he spotted rusted bed frames, crumbling bookshelves, and scattered toys left behind by children long ago. The officers checked each one carefully, but there were no signs of Maggie or any recent activity. Any footprints or evidence of visitors in the halls had already been concealed by the ever-shifting vegetation inside the manor.

The strangest sight they encountered was in an overgrown courtyard at the center of the building. Bruce paused where a mass of roots converged to form a crude archway. The tangle of thick, knotted roots pushed up through the cracked concrete, twisting over one another and intertwining unnaturally. He crouched briefly, inspecting the vines, then stood back up. Most of the roots looked dead, probably part of a play area leftover from when the place was still open. He pushed the thought aside and continued on.

The officers took their time, but after hours of searching, they found nothing. With the building confirmed empty, Bruce holstered his weapon and sighed, rubbing his fingers over his chin. He didn't like this. He didn't know what it was, but he had a strange feeling that he was missing something. But with no sign of the girl or anything out of the ordinary, he had to move on. He called Maggie's name one last time, but only the wind replied as it whispered through broken boards.

The search thorough but fruitless, the officers made their way back outside. Although they found nothing to suggest Maggie had been there, Bruce couldn't escape the nagging feeling that Eliza was right and he had missed something important.

Back at the Danvers' household, Julie followed her brother to his room and plopped down on the bed, crossing her arms while she considered the best way to broach the subject at hand. She thought of his awkward expression while being questioned by their mother and then again by the sheriff. Seeing no point in beating around the bush, she cut right to the chase.

"Why did you lie?" she asked.

"What do you mean?" Finley replied.

"To the sheriff," she said. "You told him we came inside the house together, but you and Maggie stayed out after I went in."

"Oh," they said with a nervous chuckle. "It was just a couple of minutes, and I came in right after you. I didn't think it was important."

She eyed him cautiously, trying to discern the truth from his words, but he avoided her gaze, offering little clue of his thoughts.

After an awkward silence, Finley continued defensively. "Do you really think I had something to do with Maggie's disappearance?"

Julie didn't know how to answer. The Ethan she had known her entire life would never hurt Maggie, she was sure of that. But the boy standing in front of her felt like a stranger. "I—I don't know," she said softly. "But you were the last one to see her and you've been acting strange ever since."

"I told you we just talked in the front yard for a minute and that was all," Finley retorted, showing their frustration at the implied accusation.

But Julie knew her brother wasn't telling the truth. Curiosity had gotten the better of her, and instead of going to sleep, she had watched them from her bedroom window. It wasn't just a minute. She heard the conversation and saw the kiss. She watched them walk off together down the road. She had hoped Ethan would offer a satisfactory explanation, but his repeated denials left her no choice but to play her hand.

"Where did you guys go after that?" she pressed.

"I told you already," Finley replied, their voice even. "We went inside."

"That's not true, though. She didn't go home, and neither did you."

Finley's fingers tightened into a fist. "No. You're mistaken."

Julie knew what she saw, and she didn't like being gaslit. With Maggie missing and Ethan lying about his last interaction with her, she struggled to make sense of it all. *Would he have hurt her if she rejected his further advances?* The possibility frightened her.

"Am I?" Julie said, leaning forward and calling his bluff. "Then why do you look like you're lying?"

She expected more denials. More lies. But rather than rejecting her assertion, Finley just stood there. She hated accusing her brother, but with Maggie's life at stake, staying silent wasn't an option. With her voice low, she said, "I saw you from the window after I went in. You didn't just stay outside for an extra minute. You walked down the street together, and you weren't heading toward her house."

Finley glanced up, a hardened look in their eye, and met Julie's gaze as they struggled to think of an explanation. "Oh. I forgot all about that. It was just a quick walk. It must have slipped my mind. She said she wasn't tired and wanted to take a loop around the block before going in," he offered. "She was fine when I left her. Honest."

Julie furrowed her brow. She wanted to believe him, but she hesitated, considering her options. She felt like she should tell someone, but she couldn't betray her brother's trust until she had absolute proof of his involvement. It wasn't like Ethan to lie. She wanted to keep pushing, but she wasn't getting anywhere, and something about the way he spoke gave her pause. She studied him for a moment while an unsettling feeling grew in the pit of her stomach. Something was different about him, but she didn't know what.

Finley saw the uncertainty in her eyes and sat down on the bed next to her. They reached over and pushed her hair out of her face, gently tucking the lock behind her ear. "Don't worry about Maggie," they said confidently. "I'm sure she's fine. We'll see her again soon."

Finley traced her jawline, slowly running their finger down to her chin. The contact caused Julie's entire body to shudder, sending a shiver down her spine. Her instincts told her to recoil from her brother's intimate gesture, but his touch released something in her that instantly calmed her. Her anxiety dissipated, and she suddenly had a feeling that he was right. Everything would be fine. His fingers were icicles on her skin, but the cool touch was refreshing in the oppressive summer heat. Any misgivings or suspicions she harbored faded with the contact, replaced by a feeling she couldn't put into words. She only knew deep in her bones with an inexplicable certainty that she could trust him.

Fairfield Gazzette

Early Edition   Fairfield's First Choice for News Since 1926   Vol. 32 No. 10

50¢

August 22, 2001

LOCAL CHILDREN VANISH NEAR FAIRFIELD CHILDREN'S HOME

Authorities and volunteers are searching the wooded area surrounding the abandoned Fairfield Children's Home after three local children went missing late Tuesday afternoon.

Gene and Margaret Bell reported that their twin daughters, Sarah and Elizabeth, were last seen riding their bicycles on the north side of town. Witnesses said they saw the girls riding with a local boy along the fence line of the old orphanage. A subsequent check of the boy's house determined he had gone missing as well.

Sheriff Bruce Cahill stated that search efforts have continued through the night. "We're covering every inch of those woods," he said. "We're not ruling anything out."

Residents have long considered the derelict Children's Home a place best avoided. Several recalled the original scandal tied to disappearances connected to orphans at the property before its closure in 1981. "That building's cursed," one volunteer said. "It should've been torn down years ago."

Officials have asked the public to report any information they may have that could be related to the missing children immediately.

CHAPTER 18

The search dragged on until the last of the day's sunlight slipped behind the trees, casting the town into an uneasy twilight. The people of Fairfield moved in small clusters, calling Maggie's name in the growing dark, but no answer came.

With a feeling of defeat, the searchers returned to their cars and trucks while Sheriff Cahill promised to organize another sweep the next morning. But after a full day of searching with nothing to show for it, everyone departed with somber moods and dampened spirits. The grim looks shared among the townsfolk said what no one dared voice aloud. The hope that they would find Maggie safe was slipping away.

A few neighbors lingered in the Danvers' driveway, speaking in hushed tones and stealing glances at Maggie's parents with pity in their eyes. Maggie's mother approached Mrs. Danvers with a small stack of paper. She held out the homemade missing posters with Maggie's smiling face printed in black-and-white.

"We put these up around town, but I was hoping you would take a few to hand out," Mrs. Evans said quietly, squeezing Mrs. Danvers's hand with desperation in her eyes. "Just in case."

April took the posters with trembling fingers. The photo of Maggie beamed up at her, bright and alive. The sight of her formed a cold pit in her stomach. She nodded, feeling the weight of the poor woman's worst fear coming true pressing heavily on her chest. "Of course," she replied. "We'll be out again first thing in the morning to continue looking."

Mrs. Evans offered a weak smile in return, then went back to her husband before disappearing inside the house as the stragglers took their leave.

The Danvers returned home exhausted, their faces worn and dusty from combing the woods all day. Back inside, a heavy silence clung to the air. A few hours later, April sat at the kitchen table, her hands wrapped tightly around a lukewarm cup of coffee and worry etched on her face. Across from her, Mr. Danvers paced.

"You're reading too much into it," he said again. "He's just worried about Maggie, like the rest of us. He's just... processing it differently."

Mrs. Danvers bit her lip, fighting the urge to argue. *Maybe that's all it is*, she thought. *Maybe he's just worried for his friend.* But deep down, the unease churned in her belly, whispering that it wasn't just sadness transforming her son into something she barely recognized.

She shook her head. "No, it's more than that. You haven't seen how he looks at us? The way he interacts with people? It's not normal. The way he eats, the way he walks, the way he speaks. It's off. Something's different about him. I know my boy. It's almost like he's trying too hard to be normal."

Mr. Danvers opened his mouth to argue, ready to blame his son's odd behavior on adolescent mood swings and the awkward stages of puberty, but the sound of the doorbell stopped him. April jumped in her seat at the interruption, spilling a few drops of coffee on the tablecloth. Ignoring the mess, she rose, hoping the caller brought good news about Maggie. When she opened the door, she couldn't have been more surprised to see Eliza Wilkins standing on the porch, her thin frame lost in her tattered, flowing dress.

"We need to talk," Eliza hissed. Her eyes peeked past Mrs. Danvers into the house. "Privately."

Hesitating, Mrs. Danvers glanced nervously over her shoulder to confirm her husband was out of earshot before stepping outside and pulling the door shut behind her.

"It's your son," Eliza said, skipping any pleasantries, "the one you think is living under your roof."

"What do you mean?" Mrs. Danvers whispered. "What about him?"

Eliza leaned closer. "He's not who you think he is. Trust your instincts. Watch him closely. And whatever you do, don't leave him alone with your daughter, 'less you want her to wind up like the other girl."

April couldn't believe it. Under normal circumstances she would have been furious if the old woman had come to her door with such accusations about her son. But it was almost as if Eliza had read her mind. Thoughts of her son's peculiar behavior flashed through her head. She had so many questions, but before she had a chance to ask any of them, Eliza turned and hurried away, disappearing down the sidewalk as if she had never been there.

Shaken, Mrs. Danvers went back inside.

Her husband was still pacing, oblivious to her exchange. "Who was that?" he asked. "Any news on Maggie?"

"No. It was nothing," his wife replied, wishing to avoid upsetting him further by repeating Eliza's seemingly ridiculous claim. "Just a volunteer letting us know they'll be gathering at Maggie's house again first thing tomorrow morning."

Mr. Danvers grunted in acknowledgement.

But was Eliza's claim so ridiculous? April had just finished sharing her own suspicions with her husband, then to hear the same words from a virtual stranger's mouth both validated her fears and made her realize just how absurd the whole thing sounded. Surely Ethan was still the same boy he had always been. To think otherwise would be preposterous.

Later that night, while the house settled in a tense silence, the family sat down in the living room to watch their favorite sitcom. Mr. Danvers hoped the satirical comedy would lighten the mood and be a welcome distraction from the aura of despair hanging over the town.

While the rest of the family stared at the flashing images displayed on the screen, Mrs. Danvers was unable to focus on the show. Instead, her attention remained with the children, especially Ethan, looking for any sign of familiarity in the boy.

Julie watched silently, a melancholy look on her face, while Ethan laughed at every line, even the ones that weren't funny. April knew everyone handled grief differently, and she wanted to see her children happy, but the unnatural way he bellowed at each joke gave her the creeps. Seeing the opposing mental states of her children made her realize how little concern Ethan showed for his missing friend.

Unable to concentrate on the show, April couldn't just sit quietly, ignoring the reality of the situation. "We had a long day," she said to the room. "I think I'm going to head upstairs and get some rest. Tomorrow morning will be here before we know it."

Julie glanced at her mom and nodded, while Mr. Danvers said he would be up as soon as the show finished. Ethan's gaze never left the screen, laughing along as if he hadn't even heard her.

Mrs. Danvers took her leave and crept up the stairs, pausing as she passed Ethan's room. She poked her head in and was met with the same earthy scent she noticed the previous day. The peculiar odor only seemed to have grown stronger even though she had cleaned earlier that afternoon.

She pushed the door open. The room was dim and oddly cold. Dead leaves littered the recently vacuumed floor near an open window, and the once vibrant houseplants she insisted on giving Ethan to brighten up the room were blackened and shriveled, when only a week ago they had been thriving.

She moved to the window and closed it, scolding Ethan in her mind for leaving it wide open as she knelt down to pick up the crumbling leaves. She would have to vacuum again but didn't currently have the energy for the task.

Her gaze swept across the room, looking for anything out of place. Dirty clothes lay in a heap next to the hamper, and the bed remained unmade. No matter how many times she reminded him, the boy refused to tidy up. At least some things hadn't changed. The sight of the balled up sheets spilling onto the floor gave her a strange sense of comfort. Maybe she was blowing things out of proportion. She refused to let the words of the town pariah rattle her. She had enough on her mind without second guessing her own son. Even with all of his recent changes, Ethan was a good boy. They would find Maggie safe and sound, then things would return to normal. She had to believe that.

She walked to his bed and smoothed out his sheets. As she tucked in the blanket around the corners of the mattress, a flash of silver caught her eye. Something was shoved between the bed and the wall. She hesitated, then reached into the crack and pulled it free. It was a small silver locket. She recognized it, but it wasn't Ethan's. It was Maggie's. She had seen it around her neck at dinner just days ago. So why would he have it? Normally she wouldn't have batted an eye at the forgotten chain, but with Maggie's disappearance and Ethan's peculiar behavior, seeing the locket brought new doubts into her mind.

With her heart pounding, she tucked the chain into her pocket and backed out of the room, shutting the door with a soft click. Her mind raced. Ethan's strange behavior. Eliza's warning. The smell. The dead plants. The locket.

Could Ethan really be involved in Maggie's disappearance? Surely her husband was right and

Ethan's recent disposition was nothing more than an awkward display of grief from a hormonal teenage boy. He was just processing Maggie's disappearance differently than the rest of them. But something didn't add up. Ethan's demeanor changed days before that. No matter how much she tried to convince herself everything was fine, she couldn't shake the feeling something was terribly wrong with her boy.

CHAPTER 19

The next morning, April Danvers woke up with a splitting headache. She had tossed and turned all night, listening to her husband snoring in her ear. She didn't understand how he could sleep so well with everything going on. Between her worry for Maggie and fears about what was happening to her son, she had been lucky to get a few hours of shut-eye.

Already off to a slow start, she loaded up a large thermos with iced coffee before heading out to join the search party. With the sun breaking the horizon before six o'clock, daylight was already wasting and she needed a jolt of caffeine to keep her alert.

She knew the statistics. They repeated the numbers during every news report and true-crime documentary featuring a missing child. Maggie had already been gone for more than twenty-four hours. Each minute that went by decreased the chance they would find her alive, although April couldn't bear to think of the alternative.

By the time she and her husband were dressed and joined the group across the street, some of the volunteers had already departed but the sheriff was still in the front yard, handing out assignments. The couple wasted no time in joining the day's probe.

The search party moved methodically through the woods, combing every inch of brush and undergrowth for the missing girl. April kept her eyes low, scanning the area as she went, but her mind was elsewhere, circling back to Ethan over and over. Something about his expression unsettled her: the calmness, the way he held her gaze just a moment too long, like he was studying her. Maybe it was selfish to think of her son, who was safe at home, while they were out looking for Maggie, but she couldn't help it.

She glanced at her husband, who was deep in conversation with one of the neighbors as they scoured the ground. He had brushed off every concern that she had raised as part of the boy's awkward stage, but thinking of Ethan's strange, distant expression made her stomach clench.

"Hey, hon," she said, cutting into her husband's conversation. "I'm not feeling great. I think I'm gonna head back to the car. I'll hang up some flyers in town on my way home. Can you find a ride back with someone else?"

He nodded distractedly, too caught up in his exchange to argue. "Sure, I'll catch up with you later," he said before returning to his chat.

April made her way back toward the car and drove the short distance to town, parking in the municipal lot near the post office. With the stack of missing-person flyers tucked under her arm, she headed toward Main Street. Stopping at the first bare telephone pole she found,

April held one of the flyers up against it. Maggie's face stared back at her as she struggled against the wind to affix the tape. With every flyer she hung, the sick feeling in her stomach grew.

Even with her new task, April still couldn't focus. Eliza's words replayed over and over in her head. She just couldn't escape the nagging feeling that something was wrong back at home. It was an old instinct she had learned not to ignore. Call it a mother's intuition, or maybe just nerves worn ragged from a week of nonstop stress. Unable to shake the feeling, she returned to the car, her heart racing.

She was surprised to find the house quiet when she pulled into the driveway. She didn't quite know what she expected, but from the exterior, everything looked normal. Maybe once she went inside and confirmed the kids were safe she would feel well enough to return to the others and help in the search. Until then, she wouldn't be much use to them.

The screen door creaked as she entered, breaking the stillness inside. The silence worried her. She didn't hear the usual racket of video-game gunfire or rock music or the clatter of dishes from the kitchen. She slipped off her shoes and set down her bag, listening.

"Ethan?" she called. "Julie?"

No answer.

As she climbed the steps to check on them, she heard the faint sound of water running from the bathroom upstairs. The tension eased from her shoulders when she realized why no one heard her call. Julie must be in the shower, and Ethan was probably off in his own world again.

Halfway up, she heard a faint creak, the sound of weight shifting on the floorboards.

"Hello?" she called but again was met with silence. When she reached the top of the stairs, she immediately noticed Ethan at the other end of the hallway. He was standing stoic, his back toward her.

"Ethan," she repeated.

He didn't turn or acknowledge her presence, remaining almost statue-like just outside the closed bathroom door. He had one arm against the wall, supporting his weight, and the other curled at his side. As April made her way down the hall, he moved. It was just a slight tremor. His head tilted and his arm twitched, but his gaze remained fixed on the wall in front of him. He seemed to be in another trance-like state.

She watched him for a moment, trying to figure out what he was doing. If he had to use the toilet, there was another bathroom downstairs. She called his name again, but his attention remained elsewhere. She continued down the hallway, concern for her son's mental state growing with each step she took. As she advanced, another sound caught her ear—the heavy, ragged sounds of Ethan's breath. Phlegm bubbled in the boy's throat with each raspy gasp. The repeating rattle quickened as she neared, his throat emitting noises that barely sounded human.

As she crept closer, the trickle of the shower and even the sound of Ethan's labored breathing faded away, replaced by the sound of her own pulse hammering in her ears and drowning out the noise around her. By the time she stood only a few steps behind him, she realized he wasn't just staring at the bathroom door. The door stood slightly ajar, and his gaze was fixed on the opening. April followed his line of sight to find Julie standing naked in the shower, a partially steamed glass door providing only minimal coverage. Her eyes were closed as she washed her hair, oblivious to the voyeur just outside the threshold.

April knew puberty was a weird age for young boys and being interested in the opposite sex was normal, but to find him leering at his own sister in that way shocked her. Even with his mother standing only a few feet behind him, he continued peering inside, failing to notice her presence. No matter how much she wanted to run away and forget what she saw, April was unable to allow the deplorable act to continue. She grabbed his shoulder and turned him away from his fixation, startling the boy in the process. What she saw only heightened her disgust. The boy's hand rocked back and forth, just out of view, tucked into the waistband of his unbuttoned pants. His arm jerked back and forth rapidly, stroking an enormous bulge in his underwear. Revolted, April averted her eyes but not before glimpsing a dark, black spot spreading from the center of the boy's crotch.

With Ethan's attention diverted from the shower, his eyes locked with his mother's but he made no attempt to hide or stop his perversion. He continued to stroke his bulge as a wail of revulsion escaped April's lungs.

Frozen in horror, her gaze bore deep into her son's eyes, and for a split second, she saw a flash of yellow reflected in his pupils. There was nothing of her son in the glimmer she saw. But as soon as her brain registered the sight, his natural color returned. She stared at him in shocked silence as she attempted to convince herself that what she saw was nothing more than a trick of the light. But after the horrible act she found him in, she needed a reason, any reason, to believe that the boy standing next to her was *not* her son.

The shower stopped, and Julie stepped out of the tub, finally noticing the commotion in the hall. With her mom and brother still locked in an awkward staring contest, she quickly wrapped a towel around herself and leaped to the door, slamming it shut.

"A little privacy, please!" she yelled.

April took a step backward, wanting to put as much space as possible between her and the stranger in her house. She fought the urge to turn and run, knowing she couldn't leave Julie alone with him, not after what she just witnessed.

Without another word, she headed downstairs, leaving Ethan standing in the hall. She found her purse and removed her phone. She began to dial her husband's number but stopped. What would she say? No matter how she explained it, he would just chalk it up to more teenage hormones. He would never believe the worst of her suspicions. She wasn't even sure what she suspected. *Possessed by a demon? Invasion of the body snatchers?* It sounded crazy even to her.

Not knowing what else to do, she went back upstairs looking for Julie, dreading coming face-to-face with Ethan again, but the hall was empty as if he had never been there. His bedroom door was closed. She exhaled a sigh of relief at being spared another awkward encounter with the boy, thankful he returned to the seclusion of his room.

She called for Julie, who was still in the bathroom, getting dressed. "Julie, hurry up in there and meet me in the car right away," she yelled through the closed door, urgency plain in her voice. She couldn't bear the thought of spending one more second under the same roof as her son.

CHAPTER 20

April Danvers waited impatiently by the front door, pacing back and forth in the living room while her daughter finished getting dressed. Every impulse in her body screamed for her to get out of there, but she couldn't leave Julie alone while Ethan was in the house. Luckily the boy hadn't emerged from his room since their encounter in the hall, but she wasn't taking any chances. The five-minute wait felt more like an hour.

Finally, Julie trotted down the stairs with a confused look on her face. "Mom, what's going on?" she asked as she descended. "Where are we going?"

April didn't have an answer for her. Truthfully, she didn't know where they were going. She hadn't thought that far ahead. She just knew staying at the house was out of the question. Instead of answering, she ushered her daughter outside and into the car. "Let's go. We'll talk about it on the way," she said.

They sat in the car for a moment while April decided what to tell Julie. She couldn't just rush her out of the house with no explanation. She also needed to decide on a destination. Her first thought was to return to her husband and the rest of the search party, but with children forbidden from the woods, she wouldn't know how to explain her daughter's presence. No matter how much she suspected Ethan, she couldn't levy such vile accusations against her own son in front of everyone. No one would believe Ethan was possessed, but they hadn't seen what she saw. She didn't know if he was being controlled by a demon or under the influence of dark magic, but something was very wrong with her boy.

There was only one person in town who would believe her story, someone who went through the same thing themselves only to be shunned when they sought help. Eliza Wilkins had the answers she needed. April prayed the old woman knew a way to rid Ethan of the evil living within him.

"Where are we going?" Julie repeated, frustration evident on her face.

April looked at her daughter with concern in her eyes. "I'm not sure," she replied. "But it's not safe at the house."

"What do you mean it's not safe?" Julie asked. "Is this related to Maggie? Should I run in and grab Ethan?"

"No!" April replied emphatically. Then, in a calmer tone after seeing her daughter's shock at the harsh reply, she added, "He'll be fine. I just..." April trailed off, unsure how to put the situation into words that didn't make her sound crazy.

"Mom, you're scaring me," Julie said, seeing the desperation in her mother's eyes. "What's wrong?"

"We just need to go. What about the sheriff's son? Noah. Can you go to his house for a while?"

"Uhh, sure, I guess. Let me text him to see what he's up to. But are you going to tell me what's going on?"

April sighed. "It's your brother. Something's not right with him."

Julie hesitated, thinking of her own recent interactions with Ethan. Had her mom noticed his strange behavior too?

"I have to talk to Eliza," Mrs. Danvers continued. "I think she may know what's happening."

"That old crone? I thought you always told us not to listen to her crazy stories. Do you think she could've been the one to hurt Maggie?"

"No, it's not that," April replied. "I think she might be the only one who can help."

Confused as ever, Julie gave up trying to decipher her mom's ramblings and shifted her attention to her phone. She tapped furiously for a few moments, and it pinged instantly in reply. "Noah said you can drop me off. He's hanging out with Connor while everyone is out searching."

With their destination determined, April started the car, then backed out of the driveway. She glanced at the house one last time as she pulled away. Ethan was there, watching them from his window. The child remained motionless, as if he was nothing more than a mannequin. His piercing stare met April's gaze, sending a shiver down her spine.

As they drove off, her eyes remained glued to his reflection in the rearview mirror until she turned the corner and the house fell away from view. With the boy out of sight, a sense of relief washed over her as the distance between them increased. Her daughter was safe, but the lingering fear for the fate of her son remained anchored at the forefront of her mind.

Noah and Connor were already in the driveway, tossing a football back and forth, when Mrs. Danvers and Julie pulled up to the house. Julie opened the car door and was about to climb out when her mother grabbed her arm.

"If they ask why you're here, just tell them you were bored at home," said April.

"Well, considering I don't even know why I'm here, that shouldn't be too hard," Julie replied sarcastically.

April wanted to tell Julie more but thought better of it. She knew her daughter. Anything she told her would be relayed to her friends the moment she drove off. "Just stay away from Ethan for now, okay?"

"Sure, Mom," Julie replied with a roll of her eyes. "Whatever you say."

"I mean it. Promise me."

"Okay, fine. Now can I go before Noah and Connor start asking questions?" she said, glancing down at her mother's hand, which had begun to leave a mark on her arm.

Not realizing how forcefully she held her daughter, April released her grip.

Julie pulled her arm away from her mother and wasted no time climbing out of the car. Without another word, she closed the door and joined her friends, slipping into their familiar rhythm as they tossed the football to one another.

April lingered a moment, her knuckles white as her hands gripped the steering wheel. Noah's mother waved at her from the porch. At least an adult was around to keep a watchful eye over the children. Everything looked normal.

But it didn't feel that way.

As she backed out of the driveway, she considered just returning to meet up with her husband and the rest of the search party. She almost did. But this was her chance to speak with Eliza without raising her husband's suspicion. She hated keeping secrets from him, but she needed answers and he would never entertain anything Eliza had to say. So she turned, not toward the volunteer meetup but toward the opposite edge of town, where an old woman lived in a sagging house shrouded behind a swatch of overgrown plants and an endless supply of rumors.

As she approached the unsightly property, doubts swirled in April's head. She, and the rest of the town, had always considered Eliza Wilkins certifiably insane, but with her son's fate at stake, she was desperate and out of options.

April saw the way Eliza looked at Ethan during her tirade at the search party gathering. It was as if she saw something in the boy the others couldn't. April needed to find out what that was. The woman had been certain enough to show up at their door, flinging wild accusations. At the time, April hadn't want to believe the claims, but things had changed since then. The seed of doubt Eliza planted in her mind had grown. Finding him in the midst of that depraved act was the final straw. She was ready to listen, with an open mind, to whatever Eliza had to say. The old woman was the only one who might shed any light on what was happening to her son.

So Mrs. Danvers made her way up the cobblestone walkway, stepping carefully to avoid the tall weeds emerging from between the stones. When she reached the front door, she hesitated, unsure what to say. Before she gained the courage to knock, the door swung open and Eliza stood on the other side as if she had been waiting for April's arrival.

"It's about time," the old woman said in a raspy voice. "I've been expecting you."

April swallowed before replying. "I need to know what happened to my son."

Eliza's expression didn't change, but she nodded slowly and held the door open, motioning her visitor inside. "Then you'd better come in and have a seat."

The inside of Eliza's house smelled of dried herbs and dust. Heavy curtains blocked most of the light, allowing only a few rays of sun to sneak in through the edges of each window. Clutter filled almost every inch of the main room. Everywhere April looked, she saw shelves crammed with books in varying conditions, strange charms hanging from the ceiling like cobwebs, and bundles of what looked like sage and small bones bound in twine.

Eliza led her to a faded kitchen table scattered with packing slips and shipping materials. She pushed aside a stack of padded envelopes and gestured for April to sit. "They don't like iron," she said abruptly, lighting a partly melted candle, "or salt. St. John's Wort repels them. But they've adapted, some of them. They've lived in these woods for centuries. They hide in plain sight until they have what they want and then disappear, just like with my Billy."

The fragmented thoughts spewing from Eliza's lips didn't give April the answers she was looking for. She barely knew what the old lady was going on about, but her words unlocked a memory long forgotten, urban legends she hadn't heard since she was a little girl, of strange creatures that took the form of young boys and abducted children who lost their way in the woods. She always considered the tales nothing more than folklore aimed at keeping the children from wandering off alone.

April leaned forward, her hands clenched in her lap. "You think he's a changeling? My son?"

Eliza met her eyes. "I know it."

"So what are you saying? That he killed Maggie?"

"Killed her? No. They need her alive. The girl is useless if she's dead. But you must remember, although the creature looks like your son, a boy it is not. It is something else entirely."

A heavy silence passed between them.

April shook her head. "How do we get them back?"

"You don't," Eliza said softly. "If it wears your son's skin, then it is already too late. Your boy is gone."

"No." The word burst uncontrollably from April's mouth as she slammed her hands on the table. "You don't know that. He could still be alive. If you say Maggie is alive, then he could be too."

Eliza returned April's gaze with a look of pity in her eyes, knowing she held no offer of hope for her.

"You're wrong," April continued, refusing to give up on her son. "Maybe he's just upset over his missing friend. He could be sick or, confused. He said Maggie was fine. He didn't hurt anyone."

Eliza crossed the room, pulling an old wooden box from beneath a cabinet. She opened it and removed a tattered book so fragile it looked like it might crumble. She laid it down on the table and opened it slowly, careful not to damage the delicate paper. On the page was a sketch of a wide-eyed child with pale skin, white hair, and yellow eyes. They were the very same eyes she saw in Ethan.

"They depend on disbelief," she began. "They become what you want them to be, what you need them to be. But there are signs—gaps in memory, an unnatural gaze, an absence of empathy. They aren't children. They're imposters. You already know I speak the truth. That's why you're here."

April's fists trembled in her lap. "So there's nothing I can do?"

"For Ethan? No." Eliza looked at her carefully. "But the changeling must be stopped, else more children will soon fall victim."

April stood suddenly, her chair scraping the floor. "You're wrong," she said again. "You have to be."

"I'm sorry," Eliza said. "I know how hard this is to comprehend. But you must remain vigilant. The danger has not passed. You have a daughter that needs protecting."

April's face hardened. Even if she believed something supernatural happened to her son, she couldn't accept the fact that he was dead, not when she had just seen him fifteen minutes prior. There had to be a way to save him. She turned without another word and stormed out of the house, her thoughts swirling in a violent swarm. Lost in her conflicting emotions, and against her better judgement, she got in her car and drove straight home.

She needed to see him, to touch him, anything to prove Eliza wrong.

But when she burst into the house, calling Ethan's name, she found the rooms empty. The door to his bedroom stood open, allowing the strange, earthy rot that clung to his clothes to waft into the hall. Even with the window left open again, the scent permeated the entire house.

But he was gone.

CHAPTER 21

Gene Bell sat hunched behind the wheel of his rusted pickup. He had been sitting there for the better part of the day with the engine off and the windows cracked just enough so that he didn't choke on the smell of stale cigarettes and empty beer cans that filled the small cabin.

He was parked half a block down from Eliza Wilkins's dilapidated little house, nursing a lukewarm beverage and peering through a pair of cheap binoculars he grabbed on his way out the door. His thighs were stiff, his back ached, and the vinyl seat stuck to the backs of his arms and neck. But he wasn't leaving, not until he found the proof he was looking for, anything that would prove Eliza's guilt and lead him to the missing girl. It might be far too late to save his daughters, but he'd be damned if he allowed that witch to hurt any more kids.

He tapped the dash impatiently as he watched, muttering to himself. "Crazy old bat knows more than she's lettin' on. Maybe she took the girl. Maybe she's been taking kids for years."

Finally, the curtain twitched and he saw a flash of movement inside. She was looking out the window, but not at Gene. He followed her line of sight down the road to find a car coming around the corner. It pulled up to Eliza's house and parked.

Gene looked back toward the window, but the old woman was gone. He returned his gaze to the car in time to see someone exit the vehicle. He focused the binoculars quickly, zeroing in on the visitor. It was a woman. Mrs. Danvers looked around nervously and approached the house. She seemed rattled, her face weary, as if she hadn't been sleeping well. Gene watched closely as she stepped onto the porch. The door opened to reveal Eliza. The two exchanged a few words, and the women disappeared inside.

Gene rested the binoculars on his lap and leaned back in thought. What would April Danvers want with a loon like Eliza Wilkins?

Something was going on. He didn't know how, but the Danvers woman had to be involved. He considered phoning the sheriff right away but knew Bruce already had his hands full. He needed more proof before bothering him. If he could only hear what they were talking about inside the house.

Time crawled while Gene waited for the women to emerge. The sound of a dog barking somewhere down the block formed a melody with a crow calling from a nearby tree. Gene had half a mind to walk up to the house and confront the women right then and there. But the door creaked open again, and out came Mrs. Danvers. He brought the magnifiers back to his eyes and zeroed in on her. The woman's demeanor was noticeably different from when she arrived. Her face was tight, her steps brisk and angry. She stormed down the path and back into her car. Something Eliza had said or done upset her, but what? Mrs. Danvers's hasty exit left Gene with more questions than answers.

He hesitated as she returned to her car, his fingers twitching on the keys. Should he follow her? If she was involved, maybe she would lead him straight to the missing kid. But just as Mrs. Danvers drove off and he was about to start his engine, another movement caught his eye. Eliza's front door opened again.

She stepped out into the light, hunched over and eyes narrowed, a leather satchel slung across her shoulder. She turned toward the street and began walking—not down the main road but toward the wooded trails behind the neighborhood.

Gene's heart skipped, and he muttered, "Where the hell do you think you're going?"

Dropping the binoculars onto the passenger seat, he started the engine, and shifted the truck into gear before pulling away from the curb. The tail lights of April's car faded in the other direction, but he ignored them.

Eliza was the one who needed watching.

Across town, Julie sat stiffly on Noah's couch, trying not to squirm under the smell of her friend's bad breath and the loud hum of a video game console. Connor was on the floor, elbows on his knees, furiously mashing buttons, while Noah leaned back with a bag of chips balanced on his chest.

"They're just gonna kill you again," Noah muttered through a mouthful of crumbs.

A second later, Connor died, killed in the same exact spot as his previous attempt. "You try this boss and see how far you get," he shot back as he tossed his friend the controller.

Julie barely heard them. She was curled into the corner cushion, hugging one of Mrs. Cahill's decorative throw pillows to her chest, still thinking about her mother's warning. The way she had clutched Julie's arm and looked her right in the eyes, insisting she stay away from Ethan lingered in her mind. It didn't make any sense. She hadn't said *why*. Sure, Ethan was acting strange, but did her mother really think he was involved in Maggie's disappearance?

"Hey," she said suddenly, snapping herself out of her thoughts. "Have either of you noticed anything weird about Ethan lately?"

Noah gave her a sideways look. "Define weird. I mean, he's always been kind of goofy."

Julie frowned. "I don't know. Like... different. Like he's not acting normal?"

Connor paused the game, looked over. "Honestly, I thought he was acting more normal than usual. Dude actually went inside the orphanage to get that stupid ball. That was pretty badass, kind of earned him some points."

"Yeah," Noah added, sitting up a little. "I was gonna say, he's finally starting to grow on me. Didn't think he had it in him."

Julie didn't answer. The pit in her stomach was back. The fact that Noah and Connor suddenly liked Ethan might have been the strangest thing of all.

Just then, a knock rattled the front door.

Connor looked at his friend. "You expecting someone?"

"I don't think so," Noah said as he stood and peeked through the front window. "Speak of the devil. It's Ethan."

Julie stiffened, a sudden wave of panic in her eyes. "Wait, what?"

Noah opened the door, and there he was. He looked... off, pale, tense. His hair was slightly damp and messy.

"Hey," he said, glancing at Julie. "What are you guys up to?"

Julie didn't move.

Noah and Connor exchanged a look before Noah replied. "Just hanging out. Come on in."

Ethan ignored the invitation, remaining on the front porch, his eyes never wavering from Julie.

"How did you know I was here?" she asked, returning his glare as she stood from the couch and approached the entryway.

"Where else would you have gone?" he replied. "I need to talk to you."

Julie eyed him nervously, thinking of her mother's warning.

Seeing his sister's apprehension, Ethan added, "It will just take a minute."

"Mom told me to stay here until she came back to pick me up."

Noah waved a hand. "Come on, Julie. He's not gonna bite, right? He's your brother."

Ethan tilted his head. "Of course not."

Against her better judgement, Julie stepped out onto the porch, arms crossed tightly over her chest. "What is it?"

"I need to show you something," Ethan said. "It's about Maggie. I think I know where she might be."

Her breath caught in her chest. "What? Why didn't you say something earlier?"

"Because I wasn't sure," he said. "But I went back to the orphanage. There's something there I have to show you. You need to see it for yourself."

"No," she said instantly, backing away. "I'm not going there with you."

His forehead wrinkled. "I promise. It's important," he said, his voice rising. "This could be the only chance to save Maggie."

She looked back toward the house. Noah and Connor were watching through the front window. Connor motioned a thumbs-up with a confused look on his face. Maybe her mother was overreacting. But the way Ethan was staring at her, waiting for an answer, made her skin crawl. Still, what if he was telling the truth?

"Fine," she said at last. "But we're not staying long. And if I feel weird about it or if you try *anything*, I'm calling Mom."

Ethan smiled. "Of course."

"Let me just go tell the guys that we'll be back in a few minutes."

She expected him to stop her from going back inside and demand they leave immediately, but he just nodded, smiling at her like he had nothing to hide. Maybe he was telling the truth. Either way, it was her chance to find out if he really had anything to do with Maggie's disappearance.

She went in to let Connor and Noah know that they would be back soon. After a minute, she reappeared, and the siblings headed off down the street, toward the edge of town where a broken fence and an overgrown path led to the hidden hollow of Fairfield.

Chapter 22

Finley walked beside Julie, barely able to contain their nervous excitement at the prospect of returning to the grove with another prize. The late afternoon sun had sunk behind the trees, leaving long shadows in their path. The tall pines that loomed over the road, blocking out much of the sunlight, reminded them of the dark hollow where sunlight rarely reached the forest floor.

As the pair inched closer to their destination, Finley couldn't believe their luck. They were thankful this generation held little weight in their parents' words. After the girl's mother warned her away from Ethan, they didn't think convincing Julie to follow them to the orphanage would be so easy. They had overheard the conversation. The boy's mother was on to them, and their window of opportunity was running short. Finley offered thanks to the forest spirits, relieved Julie hadn't needed to be brought back kicking and screaming. They didn't even know if that would have worked.

They weren't proud of their mission. In the short time living with her, they had grown fond of the girl. They knew those feelings stemmed from the echoes of Ethan's memories, forever imprinted in their brain, but that mattered little. Regardless of the reason, they felt a deep connection to her, even more so than they did to Maggie. They took no pleasure in knowing the girls' fate, but the survival of their kind rested upon their success. So they remained vigilant, compartmentalizing their feelings even as their bond with the human grew. They had been warned of this moment, that conflicting emotions might make them second-guess their mission. At the time, they had thought the idea ridiculous. Why would they jeopardize their quest for the sake of a human? But that was before Finley walked among them, before they learned their ways and ate their food, before they lived under the same roof. The transformation had warped Finley's mind and continued to do so. The longer they remained, the stronger the effect became. It was all the more reason to return to the safety of their grove.

The changes in them had progressed well beyond their physical appearance. Their instincts and senses had begun to shift. Human impulses they had never known had taken root inside of them. The humans' body odor, which had revolted them at first, stimulated them in ways they didn't understand. Even at that moment, the girl's salty scent stirred a strange hunger in their belly, a hunger no meal would satisfy.

They glanced sideways at Julie and inhaled sharply, filling their lungs with her scent. She looked tense, clutching her phone like it was the only thing tethering her to safety. Finley felt the tension in the air. Although the girl agreed to follow them, her guard remained high as if she knew their intent. They had the mother to thank for that, but they would proceed carefully.

As the two turned the bend, the abandoned building came into view like a blemish on the earth, its brick face crumbling and window frames faded with decay. But when Finley saw the orphanage, they didn't notice the rotting sills or deteriorating facade. Their eyes lit up at the prospect of returning home.

When they reached the fence, Finley led her to the side. "It's just through here," they said, voice soft and mindful. "I found an opening. It was actually really easy to get in."

Julie hesitated at the sight of the unnaturally twisted metal, wondering what could have caused such damage. "You're sure about this?" she asked.

Finley nodded, their face unreadable as they slipped through the fence, being cautious to avoid contact with the bent iron on their way past. "I wouldn't bring you if I wasn't."

Julie glanced at her feet and the familiar ground beneath them as she considered following her brother. The warnings ingrained in her head flashed through her mind, along with her mother's insistence to stay away from Ethan. She reeled at the possibility that he could have been the one to hurt Maggie. She didn't want to believe it. She *couldn't* believe it. But she couldn't turn back. She owed it to herself and her brother to uncover the truth. Besides, she had no way to tell Connor and Noah about any change of plans.

So she stepped through the opening in the fence, tearing her shirt as she tugged it free when it caught on the protruding metal, and followed Ethan up the overgrown path. Her brother stood just outside the entryway of the orphanage, watching her and waiting.

Satisfied she wasn't turning back, Finley pushed open the large wooden doors. The hinges groaned as they creaked open, and the building exhaled a breath of mildew and rot.

Just before entering, Julie looked up at the immense structure and swallowed, pushing back the fear creeping up her throat. She hesitated on the threshold, her heart thumping in her chest. She imagined herself stepping into the belly of a monster that had been waiting a long time to be fed.

As she peered through the doorway, she couldn't escape the feeling they weren't alone, like someone or something was watching them. She glanced back one last time at the iron fence surrounding the property, knowing she was making a huge mistake but unable to turn back, and stepped into the dark hallway. As her eyes adjusted to the darkened interior, she saw strange vines piercing through the floorboards, curling across the walls like old electrical cords in a forgotten basement.

Ahead of her, Ethan pressed on with purpose in the dimly lit hall, navigating the corridor as if he knew the intricacies of the old building as more than just a visitor. He lead her through what used to be the foyer, past a number of open doors, without giving them a second glance. While she advanced slowly, her brother kept a brisk pace, holding back his impatience as the girl dawdled.

Julie couldn't help but look into the rooms as she passed, wondering what secrets each held within. The fading sunlight that filtered through wooden planks on the boarded up windows cast a silvery glow over the dust coating every surface, revealing a pile of deteriorating and moldy mattresses stacked in the corner of one room, abandoned toys and forgotten books scattered throughout another.

Eventually they came to a stop in front of a closed door, this one larger than the others. Finley opened it and, to Julie's surprise, revealed a lush garden, overgrown with bushes, flowers, and even trees. *Has nature overtaken the building so much that it no longer looks like a building at all?* Julie looked up to see the darkening sky and realized Finley had led her to some sort of courtyard.

Tiring of her brother's games, she stopped. "Why are we here?" she asked, her voice echoing louder than she anticipated, then in a softer tone, "Is this where you brought Maggie?"

There was no point in lying. "Yes," Finley said. "I needed you to see."

"What did you do to her?" Julie demanded, suddenly on the verge of tears. "Why?"

Finley stopped and turned to her, a look of hurt etched on their face. "You were the only one who stood up for Ethan, even when it would have been easier to turn your back on him. Even when Mom and Dad were ready to give up, you never stopped looking out for him. You loved him unconditionally, and he felt the same about you. That's why our connection is so strong."

Julie scowled. "What are you talking about?"

Finley stepped closer. "Don't you feel it? The bond between us? I know you do."

She did feel something. It was an unnatural feeling that she couldn't put into words. She wouldn't dare because she would never admit it, even to herself. But she didn't have to answer because Finley already knew. The boy standing next to her didn't feel like her brother at all.

Finley took her hand in theirs and leaned in, allowing their cheeks to graze before pressing their lips against hers. Julie's eyes widened. For a moment, she didn't pull away. Her head swam with conflicting emotions, the surreal weight of being kissed by someone who wore her brother's face, even if something told her it wasn't Ethan. But then, something shifted.

Ethan's flesh flickered, almost as if a spark illuminated inside him, giving his skin a translucent green glow. She pulled away in surprise, stumbling backward, but it was gone. His face had returned to the one she had always known. She tried to convince herself it was just her nerves playing tricks on her, but she knew what she saw.

"Who are you?" she choked. "*What* are you?"

"Please, just relax. I'll explain everything," Finley begged, their voice suddenly unfamiliar and layered in an unnatural timber. "We're almost there."

Julie studied the boy who looked like her brother, attempting to glean his intentions, but his blank expression gave no clues as to his purpose. But as their eyes met, she peered past his empty stare, looking deeper into his soul, and saw something she didn't recognize. This was not her brother. But then who was standing in front of her?

Before she could react further, a voice rang out. "Back away from her!"

Eliza Wilkins stepped out of the shadows, a book held in one hand and a silver pendant clutched in the other. "Your luck has run out, changeling."

Finley snarled, baring a set of jagged teeth.

Wide-eyed, Julie stepped away from her brother, glancing back and forth between him and Eliza, who mumbled something under her breath. The words were unfamiliar, but whatever incantation the old woman spoke was working. Finley's face twisted in agony as ripples formed in their skin, and they let out an inhuman howl.

The old woman looked at Julie. "Get away from it," she called before returning to her incantation.

But before Julie had time to react, the door behind them door swung open and Gene Bell stormed into the courtyard. He kept his shotgun raised, eyes darting between Julie, Eliza, and Finley.

"I *knew* it," he barked, training his gun on Eliza. "I knew you were involved! Whatever is going on here ends now."

"Gene, don't—" she began.

"Shut up!" he yelled, his eyes wild and lip curled up in a snarl. He looked at Finley. With Eliza distracted, their appearance had settled back into the boy's form.

Finley saw their chance and pointed a trembling hand at Eliza. "She's the one. She took Maggie. She brought us here!"

Gene's hands tightened on the shotgun. Eliza opened her mouth to speak, but the gun roared to life. The shot struck her squarely in the chest, and Eliza crumpled to the ground with a gasp, blood blooming beneath her shawl.

Julie screamed.

Gene stood shaking, smoke rising from the barrel.

With everyone frozen in shocked silence, staring at Eliza as blood pooled beneath her, Finley used the distraction to their advantage. They grabbed Julie's arm and pulled her toward the center of the courtyard. "Come on!"

Unprepared to resist the sudden movement, she stumbled along behind Finley, almost losing her footing as they dragged her forward. She yanked her arm back, attempting to twist free, but Finley's grip was fierce and her struggle caused them to tighten their hold.

"There's no time!" Finley begged as they continued to pull her deeper into the foliage.

From somewhere behind them, Gene called out in confusion. "Stop! Where are you going?"

Julie barely registered Gene's call. She should have screamed for help, but everything happened so fast. Her attention remained focused on fighting Finley's pull. She continued to flounder along behind them, helpless against their grip, until she emerged into a clearing. The open area was more like a nexus than a break in the vegetation. Roots flowed from every direction, converging in the center of the courtyard into a twisted tangle of vines and branches that rose from the ground and coiled in a large circle.

In the center of the formation, the aperture should have allowed Julie to see through to the other side, but a strange texture distorted the space in a blurry haze. Within the circle, the air itself rippled as if it was made of liquid. She saw only indistinct shapes behind the waves, silhouettes blurring together in vivid shades of purple and green.

Finley continued pulling her closer to the root cluster, and before she understood what was happening, her companion disappeared into the circle, their body seeming to vanish before her eyes as they passed through. But their arm remained, still firmly holding on to Julie and dragging her forward. She gawked as the appendage dangled in the air as if it was attached to nothing at all. The strange sight caused her to freeze while her brain tried to make sense of the bizarre image in front of her. The momentary lapse in focus gave

Finley the opportunity they needed, and with another yank, she tumbled headfirst through the portal.

CHAPTER 23

Gene Bell stomped through the overgrown courtyard, searching the area frantically as he tore through vines and brush, looking for the kids. His breathing grew ragged as he choked down the thick air inside the forgotten garden. He removed his hat and wiped the sweat clinging to his forehead with the back of his arm before placing the hat back on his head.

Scanning the area slowly, he maintained a firm grip on his shotgun as he swung it from shadow to shadow. Everything about the place seemed off. He had spent his entire life in the woods surrounding the property, and he had never seen half the plant species growing in front of him. Looking around, if he hadn't known better, he would have thought he was in the middle of the Brazilian rainforest.

"Hello?" he called out. "Where'd you kids go? I ain't gonna hurt ya."

He listened for a response, or even a nearby rustle of leaves, but heard nothing.

Gene swept the area, circling the strange formation of vines that coiled like a nest in the center of the courtyard. He had never seen anything like it. He stopped in front of the structure for a long moment, wondering if the faint pulsing in the roots was merely a trick of the mind. Any way he looked at it, the vegetation's peculiar growth pattern defied explanation. He stared at the rift in the center, mesmerized by what looked like waves in the air. He walked up to the threshold and touched it, his fingers disappearing as they passed through the opening. Startled, he yanked them back quickly, pulling his arm to his chest before inspecting his hand to make sure it was still intact. He didn't understand what he had just touched, but he understood this: the children were gone.

The realization awakened memories from so many years ago when his girls went missing. The jolt rattled his mind as he remembered the outrageous claims Eliza had made. He had dismissed them as ludicrous at the time, but what if she had been right all along? He had always been so blinded by his loss that he never considered she could have been telling the truth. Shapeshifting creatures abducting children and stealing them away to a hidden world had seemed more far-fetched than an alien abduction. But the things he just witnessed made him question everything he believed for the past fifteen years, and he just blew a hole right through the only person who might have any answers.

He turned away from the structure of vines and made his way back to where Eliza's body lay crumpled on the ground. Her blood had soaked into the earth, leaving a large spot of darkened and damp dirt beneath her. He crouched beside the unmoving body and pressed two fingers to her neck. No pulse. Her eyes stared off into the distance at nothing, glassy and empty. He had killed her.

Gene stood up, his mind racing with conflicting emotions. When he found Eliza with the children, he had been certain his suspicions were confirmed. But after the gun went off, he saw something shift inside the boy; and then for him to vanish into thin air with the girl in tow... He didn't know what that boy—what that thing—was, but Eliza had been right all along. Something evil had come out of this place, and he might have just let it get away.

Sheltered by a small grove of trees just outside the wrought-iron fence surrounding the orphanage, Connor and Noah crouched low in the brush. Remaining still and silent, they shared wide-eyed glances at each other as they watched and listened to the commotion at the abandoned building.

When Julie first confessed to them her concerns about Ethan and his peculiar behavior, they doubted she was in any real danger. But when she pleaded with them to follow her at a distance while she went inside the orphanage, they didn't need to be asked twice. They had been itching to check the place out ever since Ethan showed them the lost ball. Any fear associated with the old building evaporated when they heard he had gone inside. Begrudgingly, they agreed to stay hidden unless she gave them a signal.

The boys were arguing in raised whispers about whether they should follow the siblings inside the building or keep watch from outside the fence when Eliza appeared. They stopped talking and ducked their heads low while the old woman passed. Thankfully, she failed to notice them as she slipped through the broken fence and entered the abandoned building, just minutes after Ethan and Julie. Had she been following them, too?

Then, just after Eliza passed came the unmistakable sound of Gene Bell's pickup rumbling down the road. When the boys saw him storm inside, holding a shotgun at the ready with a determined look on his face, they knew something serious was about to happen.

Only a few minutes later came the gunshot, booming from inside the building.

"We have to go!" said Noah after hearing the unmistakable sound, panic evident in his voice. "I'm getting my dad. He'll know what to do."

Connor grabbed his arm. "Wait! We can't leave Julie. We promised!"

"I'm not leaving her. I'm going to get help. You heard that gunshot. Don't be stupid."

Noah didn't wait for a response. He tore his arm from Connor's grasp, turned, and sprinted into the woods, heading for town as fast as his legs could carry him.

Connor couldn't believe his friend ditched him. Unwilling to break his promise and abandon Julie, he remained hidden in the underbrush, his heart pounding in his ears. Time slowed to a crawl. Minutes felt like hours. He wanted to go inside and help, but he was petrified of what he might find.

Knowing every second could mean life or death, he swallowed his fear and crept out of hiding, staying low as he approached the orphanage. The front doors stood open, ominous and dark, like a mouth waiting to swallow him whole. He wished Noah hadn't taken off, but at least he knew his friend would return soon with help. He hesitated, then stepped inside.

The air was heavy and damp, causing a bead of sweat to roll down the side of his cheek. Ignoring the uncomfortable heat, he continued on, calling softly for his friends as he proceeded. He walked by every room, looking for any sign of Julie or Ethan.

By the time he arrived at the courtyard, minutes had passed, and he wondered if Noah had found his father yet. The sooner they returned, the better. Connor liked to play the tough guy at school, but when it came down to it, his displays of courage were more bark than bite. He sure as hell wouldn't have gone into that creepy building to find a lost ball, especially not alone. But when it came to saving Julie, or any of his friends, for that matter, he would do what he had to.

He found the door to the courtyard and edged carefully inside. That was when he saw it. Eliza's body, or what remained of it, lay on the ground, twitching in a tangle of roots. How she became stuck in them he didn't know, but they looked like they were strangling her. As he bent down to help, he caught a glimpse of her face and stopped dead in his tracks. For a moment, he couldn't process what he was seeing. She looked emaciated, horribly so. Her sunken features went well beyond what should have been possible for someone still clinging to life.

Then he realized she wasn't. The woman's lingering movement was not of her own volition. A writhing tangle of vines gripped her torso and wound around her throat like a constrictor.

Frozen in place, Connor watched in horror as the vines pulsed against her skin, their suckers embedded deeply into her flesh, drinking her down. Her muscle sank in where they touched, her skin turning gray and papery as if her life was being siphoned out through a thousand tiny mouths.

He followed the length of the plant to the twisted circle of roots at the courtyard's center, where the vines grew thick and dark and seemed to disappear through the opening. Something pulsed there, like a slow heartbeat, and he realized the vines were alive. They were consuming her.

He blinked, certain his imagination had gotten the better of him as the woman's body decomposed before his eyes and the vines retreated into the ring of roots. He knew with cold certainty that was where his friends went.

Connor didn't give himself time to think. If he waited, fear would get the better of him, so before considering his actions, he took a step forward, then another. With a final swell of courage, he took a deep breath and, with one more step, vanished into the circle.

Knowing his father was still out leading the search for Maggie, Noah headed straight for the most likely spot to find him. Running at full speed, the boy didn't lose a step until he arrived. By the time he reached the Evans' house, the search party's meeting spot, a sharp ache shot through his side. He hunched over, holding the source of his pain, when he found his dad standing on the front lawn chatting with a few volunteers who had just finished for the day. The adults broke off their conversation when they saw the boy approach in such a hurry and waited anxiously to hear what he had to say, but Noah was so out of breath he was unable to articulate the urgency of his news.

"The orphanage…" he exclaimed between heavy pants as he caught his breath. "I saw them go in. They need help."

"Who?" his father asked. "Calm down. What are you talking about?"

"Ethan and Julie… There was a gunshot… Connor wanted to go in… but I…"

Bruce was tired of waiting for his son to spit out the rest of his story between gasps for air. "A gunshot?" he asked. "What happened?"

"It was Gene," he blurted out between breaths. "Gene Bell. He showed up. He had a shotgun."

Bruce grimaced. The last thing he needed was Gene sticking his head where it didn't belong. "Was anyone hurt?" he asked.

"I… don't know," replied his son. "I ran to find you right away. Ethan and Julie were inside. So was Eliza."

Bruce didn't like what he was hearing. "Well, what are we wasting time standing around for? Let's go."

Noah didn't need another invitation. The sheriff turned to the others and excused himself, telling them to head home and be ready for another day of searching tomorrow. But the interaction between the sheriff and his son had already drawn more bystanders, and the crowd's curiosity toward the orphanage spread.

If Gene's eyes weren't fixed into his skull, they might have popped out of his head. First, the vines came to life, right in front of his eyes. Then when footsteps approached from the hall, he ducked behind a tree just in time to see another boy come through the door. Gene recognized him immediately as a friend of the sheriff's son. He contemplated revealing himself to the boy, but before he had a chance, the kid jumped through the root structure and disappeared. If he hadn't seen the boy vanish with his own eyes, he never would have believed it, not in a million years. But he knew what he saw. He might be an old man, but he hadn't lost his mind, at least not yet.

With his hands shaking, he returned to the center of the courtyard and the strange structure erected in the middle, wondering if that was where his girls had gone. He had to know, even if he couldn't save them. Even if he never made it back, he needed closure. So he walked up to the circle and tentatively waved his shotgun in front of the opening before taking a leap of faith and stepping through.

CHAPTER 24

For a fleeting moment, Julie remained in the orphanage courtyard, and though she was amid strange foliage and dangerous company, she clung to the small comfort of knowing where she stood. But the next thing she knew, the orphanage walls fell away from view and she was striding through a lush forest, pulled along by her companion, who she was all but certain was not actually her brother.

Trees loomed overhead as she bounded through the woods, their branches bent inward, interlocking above the path and blocking out the last of the evening's fading light. The air was thick and heavy, making each breath a struggle to swallow at their brisk pace. The woods smelled of damp moss mixed with something sweet and rotten, an aroma that simultaneously enticed and revolted her.

She followed not-Ethan in silence, no longer fighting against their pull. She watched their silhouette dance in front of her, mesmerized by the shadow's rhythmic movements. The only sounds were the soft steps of her shoes on the moist ground and the buzzing of something in the distance.

Finley moved like someone who had walked that path a thousand times. At some point they had shed their shoes, and their bare feet hardly made a sound as they padded along in front of her, bobbing under branches and weaving around trees.

From behind, her companion still looked like her brother—the shaggy brown hair, the slouched posture, the long limbs that flailed awkwardly when he ran. But that was where the similarities ended. At first, Julie thought she might have been imagining it, but the differences continued to add up. Her mother's warning had been the final straw. She knew her brother would never hurt Maggie. Maybe that was why it was so easy for her to believe Ethan wasn't really Ethan. The very idea frightened her, but she kept her cool and hid her suspicion in hopes he would lead her to their missing friend.

Knowing Connor and Noah were just outside the orphanage gave her the courage she needed to accompany him inside. But now, having traveled to a strange forest, she was on her own. With each step, she considered turning around and running straight home, but she didn't even know which way that would be. At that point, following her escort was the only option. She just hoped he would lead her to Maggie. Plus, no matter how much the idea revolted her, the words he had spoken rang true. The taste of his kiss still lingered on her tongue. There was a connection between them, an attraction that was more than just sibling affection.

But something she saw amid the chaos in the courtyard had her second-guessing everything. It lasted only an instant, but what she saw in her brother's face remained seared in her memory. When the old woman began chanting that incantation, something shifted within him. It wasn't shock or fear; it was a shimmer, as if a mask made from someone else's flesh had momentarily slipped, revealing something beneath that wasn't her brother at all.

Between her overwhelming thoughts and their relentless pace, Julie didn't know how much longer she could continue. But just when she felt like she would collapse, they reached a clearing surrounded by immense trees. Many of the trees had massive trunks covered in gnarly bark that had grown into strange patterns. The abnormal contours made her want to stop and take a closer look.

Finley noticed her slowing momentum and turned to her. "We can rest up here," they said, motioning toward a large tree in the center of the clearing.

The suggestion brought instant relief to Julie, who slowed to a walk at the invitation. "Where are we? What is this place?"

Finley sat on a large root that curled from the ground, forming a natural bench, and motioned for her to join them. They looked up at her, a spitting image of her brother except that strange flicker deep in their eyes. "This is my home. It's where I was born."

"You're not Ethan," she said plainly, not a question but a statement.

"No. I took his place."

Julie didn't sit. Her heart still thudded in her chest. "You said you would take me to see Maggie."

Finley nodded. "That is true. And I will. But you have to understand who I am before you can understand what's happening to her."

"Where's my brother? Is he here too?"

Finley's composure broke. Their face told Julie what they failed to express in words.

She hesitated, dreading the answer to her next question. "Did you kill him?"

Finley broke eye contact, looking down at the ground in shame. "He died in the orphanage. I didn't kill him; the vines did. They took him and gave me what I needed to become him."

Julie shivered, holding back her tears. "You stole his face, his voice. You tricked us."

Finley stood slowly, stepping forward until they were just out of arm's reach. "I didn't want to fool you. I had to. My kind... we're few, dying. Without hosts, we are unable to reproduce. The forest gave me Ethan's memories, his body, his voice. I didn't know what he meant to you. But I do now. I'm sorry." They reached out and touched her cheek.

Julie stepped back. "What are you, then? Some kind of parasite?"

"Not a parasite. My kind are known as the sidhe, but humans have had many names for us over the centuries: fae, changeling, leprechaun, elf. We are born of the grove, genderless, shapeless; only by taking the form of a human are we able to reproduce. That's how we survive."

"So you trick people and take them away from their families."

Finley flinched at her tone. "We don't take unwillingly, not unless we're desperate. But Maggie was curious. The forest called to her. And she answered that call."

"Take me to her."

"Before you see her, you must realize what is happening to her."

Julie's eyes narrowed. "She's pregnant, isn't she?"

Finley nodded. "In a way, yes."

"And you want me next."

Finley looked up at her, finally meeting her eyes. "I wanted you because I felt something between us like nothing I've ever experienced before. You felt it too. Even when you suspected the truth, you looked past your fear. I don't know if my feelings are Ethan's lingering memories or something else. But yes, my kind needs a human willing to open themselves to us, someone willing to sacrifice everything for the good of my species."

"So your feelings for me weren't even real. You were pretending, just to lure me here?"

"No. I wasn't pretending. They began as the memories I inherited from Ethan, but they grew into something else. They're my emotions now. I didn't understand what I was feeling until I saw the hurt in your eyes, when you looked at me and realized I wasn't him, that I never will be."

Julie wrapped her arms around herself as she contemplated Finley's words. "You think I could ever love someone that killed my brother?"

"I think you already do," Finley said quietly, still holding her gaze.

Julie wanted to deny it, to scream at them. But part of her still saw Ethan when she studied them. Why wouldn't she? They still wore his face. Even worse, when she looked at them she saw someone hurting, someone reaching out and asking for help. How could she refuse a person so desperate?

Finley sat back down on the root, crossing their legs beneath them. Their eyes glowed faintly in the dim forest light. "You want to know what we are? We're the memory of the forest. We lived in harmony with nature for centuries before humans spread across the land. We lived in the trees, in the streams, in the stones. But you built fences, you laid down roads and forgot how to speak to us. You lost your connection to Gaia, the earth goddess. Eventually, you turned on us and hunted my kind to near extinction. So we remain hidden, and our numbers continue to dwindle. Now, only few of us remain."

"Why Maggie?" Julie asked, her voice cracking.

"Because she wanted to help. And because the grove chose her. As it chose you."

"Will she die?"

Finley considered the question. "She will live, hopefully for hundreds of years, although not in the way a human lives. Once a human becomes our surrogate, their body undergoes a transformation. She will be unable to leave this forest again. That is why we must protect this grove. The humans, your friends, have followed us here. They are inside this realm as we speak. We must expel them quickly if we are to stay."

The fog grew thicker as Finley finished their explanation, rolling in with the wind from between the trees. A distant rustle echoed beyond the clearing. Finley looked toward the sound. "They are coming, my kin. They won't be as gentle as I. We must move."

Julie would have preferred to rest a few minutes longer, but Finley took hold of her hand again and set off into the woods without another word. Their advance was slower this time as they traveled without a clear path. Julie didn't know if the reduced speed was for her benefit or to avoid detection. Either way, she appreciated the relaxed pace.

After a few minutes, they emerged into another clearing. It looked identical to the spot they just left, right down to the tree in the center, and Julie couldn't be sure if they had looped around to the same one.

Suddenly, she stopped. "You expect me to give up my friends, my family... my life, just to help you?" she asked.

"No," Finley said, offering a hand. "I expect you to choose. I know it's a lot to ask. But I hoped you might understand. I hoped you might feel the same thing I do when I look at you. If you stay, we can spend centuries together. But make your choice soon, before the forest chooses for you. It won't let you leave. But I can help you escape if that's your decision."

She didn't take their hand. But she didn't run, either.

Together, they walked to the massive tree, where the branches creaked overhead and the ground pulsed as if the earth itself was alive.

CHAPTER 25

The moment Connor stepped through the portal, he felt the world lurch sideways. Holding his breath, he stumbled forward and his feet left the ground. Instinctively, he put his hands out blindly to catch his fall though he didn't quite know which direction was up. For a moment, he felt like Alice falling through the rabbit hole as he tumbled through space.

Without warning, he hit solid ground.

He landed directly on his bottom, sprawled out on a grassy knoll. Though he wasn't injured, the unexpected landing gave him quite a jolt. He rested for a moment to gather his bearings as the disorientation of traveling between worlds faded.

He turned his head, blinking in fascination as the world around him came into focus. The orphanage was gone, swallowed in an instant as though it had never existed. In its place stretched an alien and uncanny realm that filled him with unease.

Above him loomed a canopy of warped trees, their gnarled branches knotting together so densely that they blotted out any trace of the sky above. The leaves' oily sheen shimmered in the fading light. A faint breeze stirred them, creating a rustle that made the forest sound alive.

The woods themselves seemed to breathe around him. He felt roots shifting beneath the moss-covered ground as if they were pulsing in rhythm to the heartbeat of the forest. In the shadows of ancient tree trunks, clusters of mushrooms swelled to the size of softballs, their luminous skins casting green and violet glows across the undergrowth. Tendrils of mist coiled between the trees, curling upward between the trunks.

Slowly, Connor stood, the damp air weighing heavily against his body. With every breath he drew, the cloying humidity carried a sweet metallic tang that clung to his throat like the aftertaste of blood.

"Julie?" he called out.

When no one answered, he swallowed audibly and looked back at the circle of twisted branches that formed the portal he traveled through. It was the only thing that hadn't changed, though now it looked like nothing more than a tangle of dead trees, any trace of its magical essence lost to the surrounding wilderness. He could only hope that when the time came, the doorway would allow him to return home. But he would have to worry about that later.

Scanning the area, he spotted a path leading away from the circle and deeper into the forest. With little other choice, he followed it, each step taking him farther away from his route home. Knowing the importance of locating the portal quickly after finding Julie, he picked up a rock and made a notch in a tree along the path to mark his way.

He didn't know how long he wandered. He was so enamored by his unusual surroundings that he soon forgot his markings and the stone slipped from his hand. For a while, he almost lost track of the reason he came to the strange world in the first place.

As he continued deeper into the forest, the terrain began to shift. The trees grew larger and their roots more chaotic. The fog thickened, shielding the path ahead until it became barely visible in the gloomy haze. With each step, Connor felt like he was wading through swamp waters, the mist floating around his body as he pressed on. Eventually, he reached a clearing centered around a massive tree unlike any of the others he had seen thus far. A peculiar green luminescence bathed the grassy area, casting just enough light for Connor to see.

Although he had yet to encounter anyone or even any wildlife since his arrival in this strange world, he crouched on the edge of the clearing, ensuring solitude before coming out of hiding and approaching the large tree. He knew finding Julie remained the top priority, but something about the tree called to him, and he had a sudden urge to rest under it for a moment.

He approached the tree, promising himself he would only stop for a quick breather. It was then that he saw her. He didn't understand how it was possible, but he knew immediately he had found his missing friend. It was Maggie.

Somehow her body had become embedded in the base of the tree, as though the bark had grown around her. The sight in front of him defied logic. It would take years for the tree to engulf her like that, but she had only been missing for a few days.

"Maggie!" he yelled, breaking into a run upon recognition.

Emerging from the tree's base, thick roots grew upward, encasing her body. Tertiary roots twisted around her, burrowing inside her wherever they could. They dug into her nostrils and entered through her stretched-open mouth. The vines dug deep into her ears and snaked up between her legs. Her eyes fluttered half-open, unfocused and glassy. Her head tilted to the side, and a trail of what looked like black sap drooled down from her mouth.

He stopped as he neared, inspecting his friend with horrific fascination.

The skin on her stomach was stretched tight and bulging, unnaturally swollen. Her flesh had turned a translucent yellowish color, exposing the inner workings underneath. What looked like dark veins shifted, slithering like tapeworms inside her belly as shimmering fluids ran through them. He didn't know if she was alive or dead, but through her distorted anatomy, Connor saw something growing inside her.

He didn't know what was happening to his friend, but he knew it wasn't good. Tentatively, he waved his hand in front of her face, though she gave no sign that she noticed his presence.

"Maggie, can you hear me?" he asked.

Although he couldn't be sure, Connor thought he saw a slight reaction to hearing her name. He reached out to touch her, but as he made contact with her coarse skin, one of the roots twitched, tightening its grip around her neck. Maggie let out a groan that ended in a pitiful whimper, and Connor yanked his hand back as if it had been burned.

"Damnit," he whispered to himself as he circled the tree. He was unharmed, but the thought that his touch could inflict pain on her frightened him. "What the hell am I supposed to do?"

He reached for her again, more carefully this time, hoping to peel one of the smaller vines from her arm. Although initially the tree didn't react to his touch, he found the small root to be tougher than it looked. The plant seemed to fight against his pull, so he doubled his effort. As he twisted with all of his might, the root only coiled tighter around Maggie until she gasped in pain. Seeing this, Connor released his hold, not wanting to cause any harm to his friend.

He stumbled back, breathing hard as he realized how hopeless the situation really was. "I'm gonna get you out," he whispered, not knowing if she could even hear him. "I'll find a way, I swear. Just hang on a little longer."

Just then, a sound echoed from deeper in the forest. Connor froze. It was the first real noise he had heard since arriving in this place. Then, out of the corner of his eye, he noticed movement between the trees at the edge of the clearing. He ducked behind Maggie's tree, keeping his eye on the spot, when a twig snapped in the darkness. Someone or something was coming.

His thoughts returned to Julie. He knew he wouldn't be lucky enough for her to stroll into view, but he could hope. Until he knew who approached, he couldn't risk exposing himself. Staying low to remain out of sight, he crept away from Maggie's tree and back to the cover of the dense forest. He crouched behind a patch of giant fungi, hoping for a glance at the visitor.

Through the mushroom's glow, he watched the clearing, unable to take his eyes off Maggie. The image of the roots pulsing around her and burrowing deep into her body remained etched in his mind. Was the same thing happening to Julie? He clenched his fists. Whatever this place was, whatever they had done to her, he would make them pay. But first he needed to figure out a way to save her and prevent Julie from suffering the same fate.

CHAPTER 26

Gene Bell moved cautiously through the strange forest, his knuckles white from the iron-clad grip on his double-barrel shotgun. From the moment he arrived, something about these woods didn't feel right. Between the bizarre plant life, unlike any he had ever seen, to the sour mist clinging to the air, to the unnatural quiet in the flourishing forest, just being there made his blood run cold.

He wanted nothing more than to go back to his garage, where he could hide from all of his mistakes and drink himself to death. He had nothing left to live for, anyway. His family was gone and he killed an innocent woman. But instead, he was chasing ghosts through an impossible forest, attempting to atone for his failures. The fact that Eliza had been right all these years was too much for him to handle. If only he had listened to her back then, instead of vilifying her, maybe together they could have saved his girls. Just thinking about the lost opportunity made him sick to his stomach. As he trudged aimlessly through an alien world, looking for kids that shouldn't concern him, he felt like he was facing a reckoning. But if that was what it would take to find peace, then he would pay whatever price was required. He just had to find them first.

It was a slow process. He was in unfamiliar terrain and had no intention of rushing in blind. The last thing he needed was to get turned around. Not to mention, he didn't know who or what could be lurking about. A short stint in the military had taught him to move slowly and methodically, scouting each area before advancing. Knowing the lay of the land could be key to surviving a life or death situation, and he was seriously out of his element.

Gene paused every few meters, scanning the area quietly to check for sounds or movement. The woods were quiet. Too quiet. He should have heard birds chirping in the canopy and squirrels scurrying between the trees, but the only sound was the low hum of the forest itself. After wandering for what felt like hours, deeper and deeper into the maze of warped trees and glowing underbrush, he found nothing. It felt like he was chasing shadows that didn't exist. The deeper he ventured, the more the forest seemed to close in around him, every step taking him farther away from the only world he knew.

He was about to turn back when a rustle to his right made him spin with the barrel raised. Ready to fire at a moment's notice, the spring-loaded resistance was the only thing holding his finger back as it twitched on the trigger.

"Don't shoot!" a voice yelled sharply.

Gene flinched, nearly firing as he searched for the source of the shout. From behind the knotted undergrowth emerged a face he recognized. The Stevens boy, Connor, crawled out from behind a bush and stood in front of him.

"Jesus, kid," Gene muttered, lowering the shotgun slightly. "You tryin' to get yourself killed?"

"I was following someone and ended up here. When I heard you coming, I ducked behind these bushes," Connor said. "Maggie's here. They've got her in the trees." The words spilled out of his mouth quickly, eager to share the news of his discovery. "I tried to free her, but I couldn't. So I was going to get help, but I got turned around."

Gene looked the boy over. His eyes were wild, and sweat plastered his hair to his forehead. Blotches of dirt and grass stained his jeans.

"Who's got her? Where?"

"Back that way," Connor said, pointing. "... I think. But I heard someone coming, so I ran. That's when I saw you."

Gene nodded once. "Then let's go see who it is. Stick close. And if I say run, you run."

They crept through the woods together, in the direction Connor had pointed. Gene led with his shotgun, Connor just behind him, both of them careful to keep the sound of their movements to a minimum. After a few tense minutes, they heard voices as they reached the clearing.

Gene stopped and raised his hand, signaling Connor to do the same. He turned back to the boy and whispered, "Is this where you found the missing girl?"

"I don't know. It might be. Everything looks the same around here."

The old man sighed and returned his gaze to the clearing. He peeked through a veil of branches into a grassy area illuminated with faint green light. At the base of a massive tree, situated in the center, he spotted two figures sitting amid the curled roots.

Although from his angle he didn't have a clear view, Gene knew right away those were the kids they had been following. Still, something about the situation felt off. His gut told him to stay hidden for a moment and let the situation play out. He looked back to Connor again, just in time to see his face light up upon recognizing his friends.

Prepared for the boy's move, Gene grabbed him and covered his mouth with his free hand just as it opened, suppressing the forthcoming outburst.

"Stay quiet," he whispered harshly before releasing the boy.

"But that's Julie and Ethan, the ones we've been looking for," Connor protested.

"Are you sure about that?" Gene hissed, causing the boy to cease his argument.

Connor remembered what Julie had said at Noah's house. She hadn't trusted Ethan either. She said he wasn't even really her brother. At the time, they thought she was just being melodramatic, but after everything he saw, he didn't know anymore. Still, what else were they supposed to do? They couldn't hide in the bushes forever.

Julie struggled to keep her wits about her. She felt intoxicated. The air was thick. Each breath dulled her senses and made her eyelids heavy. Every shadow seemed to slant at unnatural angles, every shape just slightly wrong, as if the world here was nothing more than the artificial scenery from one of those stupid video games. Roots pulsed beneath the moss like veins, fungi swelled and shrank in rhythmic sighs, and the trees whispered in a language of only their own comprehension.

And sitting before her, in the middle of this impossible place, was Ethan. No, that wasn't right. It wasn't Ethan. It was something else.

She knew she should be terrified. Deep down, she knew she should run. She should fight the creature that killed her brother with the last of her dying breath. But for some strange reason, being in that place dismissed those thoughts. Every moment she spent there, any lingering concern for her friends or her life back home faded.

The creature watched her with those familiar blue-gray eyes. The same eyes that belonged to the boy she had known her entire life, the boy she shared secrets with when she didn't trust anyone else, the boy who stayed up late with her, telling jokes and laughing until their sides hurt. But there was a calculation in those eyes that looked at her not as a sibling or even a soulmate but as a means to an end.

Julie wrapped her arms around herself, a chill running down her back though the humid air was not cold. "How can I ever trust you?" Her voice wavered. "You killed Ethan."

"I *am* Ethan," Finley said, leaning closer, their voice cracking in desperation. "He was never separate from me, Julie. I've been him the entire time. I wore his skin, yes, but his love for you... it shaped me. It made me understand true human emotion. I have his memories, his feelings. He lives on through me. When I look at you through his eyes, I feel something that neither of us are supposed to feel."

Julie wanted to scream. She wanted to claw their face and tear away the mask of her brother. Yet as she stared into his pleading eyes, her heart stumbled because she felt it too. And when their eyes met, she saw a flicker of the boy she had known her entire life.

"Why Ethan?" she whispered. "Why us?"

"Because Ethan was brave enough to enter our sanctuary when no one else would. Because we are dying. My kin, we cannot survive much longer. We are born of the hollow, bound to it. But we can't reproduce without you, without humans, without *love*. The union has to be willing. It has to be real. Otherwise, the child withers."

Julie shook her head. "You want me to bear your... your thing?"

A ripple of hurt crossed Finley's face, and for the first time, she thought she saw real emotion in their eyes. "Not a thing. A child. Our child. A child born of both worlds. Without you, without what we shared, my people will vanish from this world."

Their words were like a blanket, familiar and reassuring. But then her mind turned to her friend. "Did you say the same thing to Maggie? Is that why she followed you here?"

Finley lowered their head as though ashamed. Their fingers dug into the roots at their sides.

"We had a connection also, yes. But not like this. Ethan's bond with her pales in comparison to what he... to what *I* feel for you."

Something in Julie's chest broke. She wanted to recoil, but her body wouldn't obey. She wanted to spit in his face, but she couldn't move. Because Ethan's mouth, his hands, everything about him was still there. It was unbearable.

"Show me," she demanded suddenly. "If you're not Ethan, then show me your true face."

For a moment, Finley's expression darkened as they considered the request. Revealing their true selves to humans was strictly forbidden. But this was different. Julie was in their realm. Soon she would be one of them.

They nodded once and closed their eyes, preparing themself for the painful transition. The change began at their skin. The warm tones drained away, leaving them pale as snow. Finley winced as their limbs stretched, joints bending unnaturally in the process. They gasped audibly as their shoulders narrowed while their arms lengthened. A look of anguish crossed their face as their features hollowed out, leaving sunken eye sockets and pronounced cheekbones. Slowly, their hair drained of color until it hung like strands of fine silk. When they opened their eyes again, they glowed an unnatural yellow, with black pupils slit like a predator.

Julie's breath caught in her throat at the sight. They were grotesque. They were beautiful. And although they looked nothing like Ethan, or even human at all, Julie still recognized her brother.

"Do you see me now?" Finley whispered, their voice distorted and layered with echoes. "Will you hate me if I no longer look like him? Will you fear me?"

Julie's chest burned. She didn't answer. She couldn't.

Finley stepped closer, and the roots shifted with them, curling across the soil. "I brought you here not to trick you, not to trap you but to let you choose. You can turn back. I will let you walk away from this place. Or…" he lowered himself in front of her, hands trembling, "…you can stay. With me. With us. And be a bridge between worlds."

Julie's heart hammered in her chest. She thought of her mother. She thought of Maggie, Connor, Noah—everyone she cared about.

Her lips parted. "I don't know what I feel anymore."

Finley's strange, pale face softened. "Then let me remind you."

When they kissed her, it was not Ethan's kiss, not her brother's. It was something deeper, hungrier, a kiss that pulled her toward the center of the Earth. And she did not resist.

Beneath them, the roots of the massive tree stirred. They lifted and wound around her ankles, her thighs, her waist. She gasped into Finley's mouth but still didn't push them away. The vines coiled over her skin, cool and damp, sliding beneath her clothes. They climbed higher, weaving across her stomach, her ribs, her shoulders, until she felt the tree itself holding her in a deep embrace.

A lump formed in her throat as the roots reached her neck, curling under her jaw. She should have screamed. She should have fought. But she had no fear, no hesitation, as she surrendered to the grove and let it claim her.

CHAPTER 27

Connor couldn't sit back and watch any longer. Beneath the shade of a colossal tree, Julie lay entangled. The roots slithered around her body, coiling tighter as they began the work of binding her to the tree. Her eyes fluttered, half conscious, and her lips trembled as though she was in the midst of a vivid dream.

And beside her, no longer wearing Ethan's familiar face, sat Finley, in their true form. Their skin was pale, stretched tight over elongated limbs. Sunken eyes and bony cheeks replaced the boy's youthful features. Their hair was colorless and their yellow eyes glowed with the secrets of the grove. They sat stroking Julie's hair as the roots wound further around her torso and legs.

Connor didn't understand what was happening, but he knew it wasn't good. He wouldn't allow that thing, whatever it was, to hurt Julie.

Gene cursed under his breath.

"What the hell is that thing doing to her?" Connor whispered.

Gene didn't answer. He removed a hunting knife from a sheath on his belt and handed it to Connor. "You circle around to the other side and be ready. On my signal, free the girl and get her out of here."

"What about you?" the boy asked.

"Don't worry about me. I'll be right behind ya," Gene replied. He raised the shotgun, eyes narrowed, waiting for Connor to confirm the plan. When he began moving into position, Gene turned toward the creature and emerged from the shadows.

"Put her down," he called out, stepping into the clearing.

Finley's head jerked up, a look of surprise blooming on their face. Their eyes glowed a faint yellow in the dim forest. "I mean her no harm. She is here of her own free will," they said. "Tell him, Julie." Their voice carried strangely, an inhuman resonance in the tone.

Julie nodded in agreement, a faraway look in her eyes. Gene waited for her to speak, but she remained silent. He pointed the shotgun to the air and pulled the trigger, setting off a loud boom that echoed through the trees. The vines retreated slightly, and she jolted awake. Julie shook her head and blinked rapidly as if just rousing from the midst of a dream, confusion evident on her face.

"Ethan?" she asked weakly.

"That's not your brother," Gene yelled. "That thing ain't even human."

Finley stood and faced the old man, turning their full attention to him with a look of irritation on their face. They glided out of their nest as if floating, the vines gently guiding them to the ground. With every tender movement, the roots shifted around Finley's feet, parting for each step they took. "Gene Bell. I don't believe we've had the pleasure."

Gene snarled and stepped forward, his arms rigid as he held the shotgun as steady as his shaky hands would allow. "You stole my life, my daughters. You robbed me of everything, my chance for grandkids. Even my marriage eroded because of you."

With Gene ready to pull the trigger at any moment, Finley smiled knowingly as if they weren't a twitch of the finger away from being blown apart. "I understand your frustration, and for what it's worth, I'm sorry about the pain you've gone through, though I could hardly be held accountable for your daughters' disappearance. I had yet to be born, after all. But the forest has shown me these things as if I were there. The truth is, we did not steal your daughters. Like Julie, they came to this place of their own accord."

"Bullshit!" Gene roared. But he didn't pull the trigger. "How dare you talk about my girls as if you knew them."

"I did know you girls, and I still do. I'm not your enemy, Gene Bell," Finley said. "In fact, I'm the opposite. I'm your kin."

Gene sneered at the thought. "You ain't no kin o' mine," he spat.

"Oh, but I am," Finley replied. But this time their voice sounded different. It was a voice Gene hadn't heard in decades but would never forget—the voice of his daughter.

"H-h-how?" Gene stammered.

"Your daughters disappeared from your world many years ago, but they lived on, in this realm. They bore a child in this world. That child was me. Your blood runs through my veins."

The revelation struck him like a blow to the head. Suddenly, he felt the world spinning around him. Gene faltered, and the barrel of his gun dropped. The creature was lying. It had to be. He refused to believe a word from that thing's mouth. His hands shook. His throat worked as if trying to form words, but none came.

"I would never lie to you," they pleaded as if reading Gene's mind, the creature's voice still imitating the tone of his long-lost child. "Your daughters were kind to me. They named me. They are my mothers. You want to know what happened to them? Do you want to see them? I can show you."

Gene took a step back. The gun wavered. He didn't know what to believe, but this was his opportunity to keep the creature distracted while Connor escaped with the girl. Not to mention, if there was even the slightest chance the creature was telling the truth... Well, he had to see for himself.

"Fine," he growled. "If they're still alive, lead the way."

While Finley's attention was fixed on Gene, Connor slipped around the edge of the clearing. Keeping low, he crept toward the rear of the tree where Julie was ensnared. When he approached, he noticed the roots had continued their work during Gene's distraction. It wouldn't be easy to free her.

He whispered to her as he reached for her arm. "Julie, it's me. I'm getting you out of here."

Her eyes flickered open at the sound of his voice. She tried to speak, but a root had already found its way into her mouth and only a faint rasp came out.

Connor tugged at the root creeping down her throat. At first it resisted, and the vines around her chest tightened further, causing him to remember Maggie's cries when he had pulled too hard. But these roots had not yet completed their assimilation. He pulled again, and the vine released its grip, sliding out of her mouth, coated in a black sticky residue.

With her airway cleared, Connor withdrew the knife and worked his fingers beneath the pulsating plant around her waist. Prying slowly while carefully sawing with the blade, he peeled the root away bit by bit until it loosened just enough to pull Julie free. She gasped, coughing as the vines released her, and fell to her hands and knees. Her chest heaved as she cleared her throat and regained her composure.

Finley couldn't have missed the commotion, but they ignored it, keeping their attention fixed on Gene and his shotgun. They spoke back and forth animatedly before the pair walked off into the woods, with Finley leading the way.

Connor bent over and rubbed Julie's back, attempting to ease her discomfort. When her breathing returned to normal, she looked up at him, still in a state of bewilderment.

"We have to go. Quickly, before that thing returns," Connor said, urging Julie to her feet.

He didn't know if she heard him, but the words anchored him to the task at hand, keeping him focused on the mission. He remembered what Gene had said. As soon as he freed her, he was supposed to get Julie out of there and back home, even if that meant leaving the old man behind. Connor didn't like returning without him, but Gene could take care of himself.

With Julie's body still weak and trembling, Connor braced her as he dragged her away from the tree and out of its grasp. Julie stumbled and her legs gave way, but Connor caught her. "Come on, Jules. Stay with me," he whispered as he pressed forward, continuing to support most of her weight.

Finally, after a nervous minute, Connor pulled her out of the clearing, breathing a sigh of relief as they disappeared into the undergrowth. He didn't look back as he circled around to the path that he hoped led to the portal home.

Chapter 28

Connor threw open the front doors of the orphanage and stumbled through the threshold, crashing onto the dilapidated wooden porch, with Julie in tow. He didn't know how they had found their way back to the portal. Maybe it was dumb luck, but it felt almost as if the forest guided them on the path home.

Beads of sweat rolled down their foreheads and dampened their hair. Streaks of mud, blood, and the black residue of the forest's roots smeared their faces and stained their clothes. Julie's eyes were wide and glassy, darting in every direction as if she expected the trees to reach out and drag her back.

The sudden brightness of the sky struck them both. After what felt like hours wandering in the oppressive darkness, the noonday sun was blinding. Connor shielded his eyes with one hand, his other arm clamped around Julie's shoulder. He knew they had been in the woods for a couple of hours, but had they really been gone that long?

"Over there!" a voice shouted.

Within seconds, they were surrounded. It felt like the entire town appeared out of nowhere, clamoring to see. Sheriff Cahill pushed his way to the front, yelling for everybody to give him room. Noah weaseled his way in after his father, glad to see his friends were okay. Behind them, parents, deputies, and neighbors who had joined the search crowded around the porch stairs, jockeying for position.

Among them, April Danvers pushed her way through, her face going pale upon seeing the state of her daughter. When she reached her, Julie nearly collapsed into her arms.

After the initial clamor, the chatter died down and an uneasy silence came over the crowd. A lump rose in Connor's throat. Everyone's eyes bored into him. They expected answers.

"Where have you been?" Sheriff Cahill asked urgently. "Where's Ethan? Where's Gene? Where's Maggie?"

Connor's lips moved before the words formed. "They're... still in there." He pointed back toward the orphanage doors, his hand shaking. "We found her. Maggie, I mean. I tried, Sheriff. We tried to get her out, but..."

"What do you mean still in there?" Cahill barked. "When Noah told me what happened, we came here straight away. We searched every inch of that place from top to bottom. The place is empty. "

"No," Connor replied, his voice cracking with desperation. "Not here. Not in this world. There's something inside that house, a doorway. It takes you somewhere else. To a forest. It's alive, Sheriff. The ground, the trees, everything. They've got Maggie. Roots, vines... they're..."

He stopped when he saw the looks on their faces. They all wore a mixture of confusion and disbelief. A few of the younger deputies exchanged condescending glances as they attempted to hold back smirks, but then he spotted Ethan's mother. Her expression differed from the rest of the crowd. She believed every word. She had seen enough of Ethan's peculiar behavior to know something unnatural had happened to her son.

"What about Ethan?" she asked hopefully. "Was he with you?"

Connor's jaw twitched, dreading having to tell Mrs. Danvers what he saw happen to her son. "Yes, no, I don't know. I saw him, but it wasn't Ethan. He changed into something else, something not human."

The sheriff sighed heavily, removing his hat and running a hand through his thinning hair. "Son, you've been through hell. I get it. You're tired. You're scared. But don't start spinning ghost stories when what we need is facts. Did you see where Maggie went? Did you see Gene?"

"I did," Connor insisted, his voice breaking. "I saw Maggie. She's alive, but they've got her. She's... she's part of that thing now. And Gene..." His voice faltered at the memory of Gene's expression as he walked off with Finley. He swallowed hard. "He stayed behind to find his daughters."

A murmur rippled through the crowd. People whispered to each other, their eyes stricken with fear and disbelief. April clutched Julie tighter, rocking her slightly and whispering soothing words into her ear.

"Sheriff," April said, her voice trembling but steady, "something unnatural is happening here. You've seen it. I know you have. Don't stand there pretending you haven't. We just watched those kids come out of a house you claimed was empty."

Bruce froze. His jaw tightened and he felt the urge to argue, but he had no alternative explanation to offer. He had always felt something was off about the orphanage but had seen nothing to suggest supernatural forces at work. Even during the original case so many years ago, when Gene's girls went missing, he had refused to give Eliza's rantings any true credence. But with Connor and Julie standing before him like survivors of a war, he couldn't deny it any longer.

Finally, he replaced his hat and said quietly, "Then we've got a bigger problem than we ever imagined."

The smiles on everyone's faces disappeared, and an uneasy silence hung over the group. Maggie was still missing. Gene was still gone. And Ethan...

The sheriff's eyes darted back to the open doorway of the orphanage and then to Connor. "I hate to ask you this, but if even a sliver of what you said is true, then I have to see it. Show me how to get to them."

Connor looked at him grimly and nodded. "It's in the middle of the courtyard. You can't miss it."

The forest grew stranger the deeper they went. Gene followed Finley through a winding maze of trees whose trunks grew twisted in ways he had never seen, their branches knitting together so tightly that no sky showed through. The thick canopy above only exacerbated Gene's disorientation. He had lost all sense of time and direction. Minutes, hours, or days could have passed since he first wandered into that cursed place. He knew only one thing. The creature was leading him somewhere, and for the first time in as long as he could remember, Gene felt a sliver of hope.

Stumbling along after Finley, Gene's boots dragged on the thick moss, while Finley moved with ease, like they had walked the route a million times. Carried by their long limbs, which looked feeble enough to snap at any moment, the pale figure glided over the rough terrain as if propelled by the ground itself. Every so often, they glanced back at Gene, and though their features were alien, Gene saw something familiar in the tilt of their head.

"You've waited long enough," Finley said softly, seeing the growing trepidation on Gene's face. "Come. They're just ahead."

The words gripped Gene's heart. Was he really about to be reunited with his daughters? His pulse hammered as he stumbled faster, pushing past vines that tugged at his jacket and ignoring the branches clawing at his face.

Finally, the path opened into a wide clearing, and Gene froze.

At its center stood a tree unlike any he had ever seen. It towered over the grove, its trunk thick and knotted with giant root nodules at its base. Deep grooves scarred the tree's surface, layer upon layer of unevenly grown bark covering the trunk. Translucent roots sprawled outward in every direction, pulsing faintly as if alive, their veins carrying a dark current inside.

The air was still, as though the thick vegetation blocked the wind from every direction. And inside the tree... Gene's breath caught in his throat. He staggered forward, his shotgun slipping from his hands and falling to the mossy floor.

Within the gnarled exterior of the tree, he saw faces, two of them pressed into the bark itself as if the tree had swallowed them. Their eyes were closed and they were still, but he recognized them instantly. He knew them as he knew his own reflection.

"Sarah... Liz..." His voice broke on the names as he rushed to them.

Their faces, though no longer human, still held their resemblance to the young girls who went missing so many years ago. Even with their skin hardened and fused into a rough bark, their youthful features remained preserved, frozen in time. Seeing them again after all of those years caused the memories to come flooding back. He pictured the two young girls in sundresses, running barefoot across the yard, hair tangled in the wind, laughing at some secret game. He remembered them as teenagers, rebellious and fiery, rolling their eyes at his advice and slipping out after curfew. Then, the night they went missing—taken from him and thrusting his life into a never-ending nightmare.

And here they were after he had all but given up. Gene pressed his palms against the bark, tears spilling down his face. The tree was warm beneath his touch, and beneath that warmth, he felt a heartbeat. It thudded slowly and steadily, in rhythm with his own.

"I found you," he whispered, choking on the words. "Daddy's here."

Finley stood beside him, a blank expression on their face. "They are of us now. The grove holds them, preserves them. They are part of the root. They endure."

Gene turned to them, anguish carved into his face. "There's no way to free them, is there?"

Finley's eyes glowed faintly, their head tilting with something almost like pity. "No. But you can join them. You can stay. The grove will take you as it took them. And you will be with them for eternity."

The thought should have terrified him. Instead, he felt immense relief. To return home empty-handed, to live out the rest of his days haunted by empty bedrooms and cold meals was no life. But here... here were his girls. He would not abandon them again.

He didn't need to answer. The choice was clear, and the roots had already started to shift across the moss, writhing like a nest of snakes.

They slithered toward him, curling around his boots and legs. Gene didn't move. He spread his arms wide and leaned into the tree as though welcoming an embrace.

The roots pierced his trousers and slid into his flesh. He gasped in pain but did not fight it. More vines rose from the ground, latching onto his torso, his arms, his neck. They lifted him upright, pinning him against the bark beside his daughters. The wood seemed to soften under him, swallowing him inch by inch.

Pain seared through his body as the roots dug deeper, siphoning everything he was. His skin sagged and his lips cracked. He felt himself shrinking. But through the agony, he saw one of his daughters' eyes flutter open. Her clouded gaze fixed on him for a moment before she went back to sleep.

"Dad," he thought he heard. Or maybe it was only the sound of blood rushing in his head.

Gene smiled through his tears. "I'm here, girls. I'm here."

His body gave way, collapsing inward as the roots drank him dry. His flesh shriveled, his bones softened, until he was little more than a husk fused to the bark. The tree pulsed once, satisfied, and stilled.

Finley watched in silence, their inhuman features showing no emotion. After a long moment, they turned away, leaving Gene's remains to become one with the grove, forever bound to the daughters he refused to leave behind.

CHAPTER 29

Finley's elongated legs allowed them to move briskly through the forest. It felt good to stretch their joints after being confined inside the body of a human for so long. But they had no time to sit and relish the return of their true form. The children had escaped. They had allowed it to happen. It was the only way to prevent more humans from entering the hollow. Their kin would be displeased, but they had little choice. The grove must be protected at all costs. So they pushed on, knowing their brethren waited in the mound for news of their return.

The deeper they traveled into the forest, the thicker the vines grew, until they walked inside a twisted tunnel constructed entirely of roots. Bioluminescent fungi grew inside the walls, lighting up the path ahead in shades of green and blue.

They darted through the narrow passageways without hesitation, their long limbs moving in strange, graceful arcs, until they reached the oldest section of the grove. The tunnel opened up into a room, though it more closely resembled an underground cave. But the chamber was no cavern, nor was it a hall. It was a hollow formed entirely of roots.

Thick branches curled upward from the earth and downward from the canopy, knotting into walls and forming a vaulted ceiling overhead. The floor pulsed faintly as though a beating heart lay somewhere below. The air inside the hollow was hot and damp and smelled of soil.

They were not alone.

As Finley entered the chamber, figures emerged slowly from the shadows. Pale as bone, with elongated limbs and sunken features, their kin regarded them with eyes the color of sulfur and ash. Each face was slightly different—some smooth and childlike, others lined with cracks and tough as bark. But all carried the same desperate urgency for good news.

"You've returned," one of them said, their voice dry and raspy.

Finley bowed their head. "I have."

The others closed in around them, their movements slow and cautious. Whispers passed between them, echoing strangely off the root-walls.

"You were careless," another hissed. "You risked much, leading the humans here."

"It was necessary," Finley replied. Their voice remained steady, but their yellow eyes flickered. "Had I not returned, I would have been discovered."

"So you put the entire grove at risk to save yourself?" another spat.

One of the elders stepped forward, their form brittle and skin stretched so thin it looked like it could tear open at any moment. "Then we abandon this grove. We move north, to a new hollow. It has been done before. We cannot wait here to be hunted."

"No," Finley snapped. "We cannot leave. Not yet."

Another kin leaned forward, their jaw hanging slightly open, revealing dark gums. "Why? Why linger? The grove is exposed. If we stay, we remain in danger."

Finley's throat tensed. "Because she carries. Maggie. The roots have taken her. The child is nearly ready."

"She is close?" one whispered.

"Closer every hour," Finley confirmed. "But more than that," their voice softened, "the other girl, Julie, she carries as well."

Murmurs rippled through the crowd.

"Impossible," one of the creatures hissed.

Finley's jaw clenched. "It is true. I planted the seed myself."

"But without the grove's nourishment, the child will wither," another said.

The murmurs turned to a loud chatter until an elder raised their hands and the others quieted down.

"The child will survive without the grove... for a time. But Finley is correct. We cannot leave," said the elder. "To abandon such fruit would be wasteful."

"To stay is dangerous," another countered. "The humans search already. If they come here again, if they find us..."

"They will not," Finley declared confidently. "The portal has weakened. Already it shrinks. Soon it will crumble, and their path to us will be closed."

A long silence followed as the others considered the implications of Finley's actions.

"You would close us off?" one of the creatures asked.

"This matter should have been decided by the elders," another hissed.

"I had no choice. Had I not acted, the humans would be here, even now. There would have been no time to escape," Finley said. Their golden eyes glimmered faintly in the chamber's dim glow. "When it is time, we will rebuild the portal. We will return for the child when it ripens. Nothing will keep us from it."

The silence broke into murmurs of agreement. The elders bent their heads, one by one, accepting that the decision had already been made. They would bide their time in hiding, but eventually they would emerge to claim what was rightfully theirs.

And beneath their feet, the pulse of the forest quickened as the grove closed its doors.

Sheriff Cahill stepped through the orphanage's ruined doorway with the weight of the entire town on his shoulders. The place reeked of decay and mildew, the smell clinging to the air. The other deputies hesitated outside the threshold, muttering among themselves, too uneasy to follow him in. Meanwhile, his son's friend Connor, who looked like he had just emerged from the grave, didn't falter to lead the way.

The boy took him straight to the courtyard.

Cahill had searched the area already and found the strange root structure but saw no magic within. Neither did he find any trace of Eliza's demise, for the blood-stained leaves had already been concealed by the time he arrived.

The sheriff's boots crunched over brittle leaves as he entered the open square. Something had changed and was still in the process of changing. The vines and moss that strangled every inch of the orphanage walls were moving. The long tendrils shriveled in on themselves, as if recoiling from a fire. Their vibrant-green hue bled out of them with startling speed, fading to gray, then black.

"Jesus," Bruce whispered, instinctively tugging the brim of his hat.

The pair stood there, helpless, as the vegetation collapsed inward. Thick roots split down the middle, flaking away to ash. The great circle of living wood, once a gateway to another realm, gave one final twitch, then cracked open and crumbled to the ground. A sudden gust of wind took much of the debris in a swirling spiral.

Bruce and Connor watched in silence as the plant life fell away. In less than five minutes, the lush garden was nothing but barren stone and dirt. Beyond the courtyard, the entire orphanage rumbled as the structural integrity gave way. Without the vines and roots to hold the walls in place, they too disintegrated.

Connor swallowed and looked up at the sheriff, the panic evident in his wide eyes as chunks of plaster fell to the ground beside them. Bruce grabbed the boy and pulled him close, shielding him from the falling debris. The thunder of the collapsing building drowned out the gasps of the crowd waiting outside, who feared the pair crushed beneath the rubble.

But kneeling in the center of the open courtyard, they huddled together as one until the dust settled. The sheriff thought of the names that had been whispered through the town and the ones who had been lost: Maggie, Ethan, Gene, even old Eliza Wilkins, who may not have been as crazy as everyone had liked to believe.

There were so many questions still unanswered and bodies that would never be recovered. His chest ached with the weight of it. But they were gone, swallowed whole by the orphanage itself.

He crouched and ran a hand through the cold, dry earth where the roots had once grown. He saw nothing but dead soil. Slowly, he rose, removing his hat as though in church. He muttered a prayer under his breath—half for the lost, half that the town finally found an end to its suffering.

He turned back toward the crowd, shoulders heavy but his face firm. Outside, the search party waited with anxious faces. Though he didn't have good news to share, maybe, just maybe, this was the final chapter in the town's long nightmare.

EPILOGUE

TWO YEARS LATER

Julie Danvers knew deep in her bones that she would never be safe. No matter where she went, no matter where she hid, one day Finley would return for their child. She was sure of it. But even with that inevitability, she had no intention of staying in Fairfield, waiting for that day to come. So she did what any parent trying to protect their progeny would do. She ran.

She gave birth just after her fifteenth birthday, and six months after that she had squirreled enough money away to leave Fairfield behind, moving far away from the orphanage's long shadow. Still a teenager herself, and with a child to boot, she struggled to make ends meet. But she found a city where trees were scarce and away from the pulse of the forest.

There, she found comfort in the sounds that aggravated others. The sirens in the street, voices bleeding through walls, and the pedestrians outside her window at all hours of the night gave her the illusion that she was not alone. The building she chose was built from concrete and steel, the plot below paved and repaved so many times that nothing should have been able to grow there.

She was a needle in a haystack, in the heart of a crowded metropolis, where the noise never stopped and neighbors were just a paper-thin wall away. She convinced herself that the sidhe couldn't reach them there. Not with traffic constantly backed up in the street and sirens screaming outside her window. There were people around every corner.

Yet she never let her child out of her sight. They were pale, with a complexion that no doctor could explain. Their hair held no color, not even blond, with large eyes, yellow and luminous, that reflected light in a way that no other child's did.

Julie kept them tucked away inside the apartment, with the blinds drawn and the locks bolted. She rarely left the house, only venturing outside when necessity called. Visitors were turned away, and she paused with bated breath whenever a passerby lingered too long in the hallway outside their door. She couldn't risk a stranger's curious glance at their colorless hair or to notice their yellow eyes that seemed to glow in the darkness.

Sometimes she caught the child staring off into space in a trance-like state, humming a familiar tune that she couldn't quite place. It stopped the moment she spoke their name.

"You shouldn't do that," she said, trying to keep her voice calm.

"Why?" they asked curiously. "It helps me remember."

"Remember what?"

They tilted their head as if listening to something she could not hear. "Home."

Every night before she slept, she salted the windows and doors, pouring a careful line from the glass jar she refilled weekly. The boundary gave her peace of mind though she had no proof that it worked. But the ritual provided her with a sense of purpose, a feeling that she was actively fighting back against an inescapable future. She could only hope her efforts would keep the roots at bay.

But no amount of vigilance could keep them out.

The night it happened, Julie dozed on the couch, as she did most nights, gripping a knife in her lap and guarding the front door with her life. She woke to the sound of splintering wood and cracking plaster. She bolted upright and sprinted down the hall, her heart pounding in her throat.

The smell of damp soil hit her senses, bringing back memories of the orphanage and the roots that had once bound her. She knew immediately that they had returned. She barreled through the doorway to find the walls overrun with vines. Roots crept up through the vents and burst through the aging plaster walls. Writhing like a live electrical cord, they spread across the floor, twisting into patterns that pulsed with a dull light.

She stared in shock as the vines weaved together before her eyes, forming an arch that mirrored the gateway in the orphanage courtyard. She screamed her child's name, but the portal had already formed, an opening that was not a tear in the fabric of time but an aperture grown from living things.

When the doorway was complete, a shimmering hole of darkness formed in the center and her child stood before it, inching closer with glassy eyes as if sleepwalking through a dream.

A pale figure emerged, but it didn't reach for them or entice them to follow. It waited patiently, as it had done for years.

"No!" Julie screamed, throwing herself across the room. "Please, don't take them!" she begged, lunging toward the child.

Julie grabbed the child's wrist in a desperate attempt to prevent their taking, but they slipped from her grasp, drawn forward by an invisible force.

The figure bowed its head, almost reverently, as it claimed what was always theirs. She understood that then. This wasn't theft. It was the fulfillment of a prophecy and nothing she did could have prevented it.

A moment later, they disappeared into the darkness, vanishing as if they were never there. The roots withdrew with them, sealing the portal as neatly as it had opened. She intended to follow them through, diving into the opening after them to no avail. The glow dimmed, the smell faded, and the walls fell silent. By the time she reached the doorway, the vines were already decaying, crumbling before her eyes.

Julie collapsed to the floor, grasping the dead roots in her fists. She pressed her forehead against them, rocking back and forth as the city outside carried on. She had hidden in the crowd, but it hadn't mattered. Her screams of anguish never even reached the neighbors, dissolving into the melody of the night. The sidhe had come back for what was theirs. Her child was gone.

By morning, only a few shriveled vines remained, brittle and crumbling to dust when she touched them. The city woke around her, uncaring of her loss.

Somewhere below, traffic roared, a neighbor laughed, and life went on.

But not for Julie. Life would never be the same for her. She would return to Fairfield empty-handed. She would wander the grounds where the orphanage once stood, desperately searching for a way back to the hollow until she became the outcast in the forest that the next generation of children whispered rumors of. All the while, she knew in her heart that her child was gone. She would not find what did not want to be found.

Acknowledgements

Gonna keep this short, so I'll start off with thanking you for reading!

Shout out to my editor, Heather Ann Larson, for making over 1,200 edits and comments and attempting to get me to stick to the rules.

My beta readers Sheryl Policar, Jordan Triplett, & Amie Kaplin for helping me fine-tune the story.

Ravynne Black for narrating the audiobook.

Thanks to everyone who has read, reviewed, or posted about any of my books.

Everyone in the indie horror community for supporting each other like family.

My kids for keeping me sane while simultaneously driving me insane.

and special thanks to my wife Amellia for putting up with my bullshit.

About the Author

LM Kaplin lives in upstate New York with his wife, two children, and an adorable maltipoo. He has been a horror enthusiast in all forms his entire life. His morbid obsession with the macabre started one night while watching Poltergeist as a young child. The next morning, he began searching for ancient burial grounds in the backyard. Dismayed at not uncovering any evil spirits, he buried his own demons for future generations to find. It's time to start digging them up.

His other works include the psychological thriller, Mine, the cosmic occult horror, Usher of the Fallen, and Fang Fiction, a collection of vampire stories.

Find him on Facebook or Instagram or email him at LMKaplin@gmail.com

Publisher's Note

Thank you for reading The False Child by LM Kaplin. We appreciate your support.

If you enjoyed this book, please consider leaving a review on Amazon, GoodReads, or your favorite social media platform.

Broken Brain Books is an indie publisher dedicated to helping authors share their stories with readers around the world. Please visit our website for more information about our releases and signed copies of our books. www.brokenbrainbooks.com

Also Available by Broken Brain Books
Usher of the Fallen by LM Kaplin
Mine by LM Kaplin
Fang Fiction by LM Kaplin
We All Fall Before The Harvest by C.M. Forest
Pacheco Pass by Aaron Lebold
Rorschach by Aaron Lebold

Anthologies by Broken Brain Books
Screams From Outer Space
Screams From The Bayou
Screams From The Ocean Floor
Screams From Beyond The Veil
Screams From The Dark Ages
Books of Horror Indie Brawl Anthology